The Chimney Still Stands

Tammy Snyder

This book is a work of fiction. Names, characters, places and incidents are the product of the author's imagination or are used fictitiously. Any resemblance to actual events, locales, or persons, living or dead, is coincidental.

Copyright © 2010 Tammy Snyder

**2018 Revised Edition

ISBN-13: 978-1468112146 (Print)

All rights reserved. No part of this book may be reproduced in any form or by any electronic or mechanical means, including information storage and retrieval systems, without permission in writing from the publisher, except by a reviewer who may quote brief passages in a review.

Cover photography, with permission, by James Stewart/Flickr

DEDICATION

For my wonderful husband, Tim, whose unwavering love and faith keeps me going. I love you!

For my three terrific sons Dalton, Logan, and Reed who always remind me there are answered prayers. Love you guys!

To all friends, family, and acquaintances; the historian at the National Park Service headquarters in Harrison, AR; James Stewart for your wonderful cover photograph; and all others who have offered their advice, help, and encouragement, I thank you.

And, finally, to those who have spent precious time with me sharing their historical experiences and raw emotions, you all helped me capture the passion I sought for my characters and I truly thank you.

The Chimney Still Stands

Tammy Snyder

PROLOGUE

"It has to be around here somewhere," Tandon Bowman muttered to himself as he drove on slowly, searching for any sign of the old drive that would lead to what he had once called home.

Out of habit Tandon checked the rearview mirror for traffic, a futile gesture on this backcountry dirt road, he knew, but whereas he expected to see a copied image of the road behind him, he was startled instead by his own magnified image staring back. He must have bumped the mirror when he had loaded the passenger seat with his luggage earlier that morning, he realized.

Tandon had finished packing the night before. Having brought enough clothes to last roughly three days, this morning all that was needed was to pack some food for the trip and get showered and dressed. The amount of light in his bathroom was fairly dim, with no window and only a low watt bulb above the small mirror, it has been just sufficient enough for him to safely shave and comb his hair. From what he could tell that morning he hadn't looked too bad.

He wasn't all that concerned about his looks anyway. Until recently, he had thought he looked pretty good for a guy in his mid-sixties. It wasn't overblown vanity that had decided on that verdict either, but merely a strong sense of self awareness.

Growing up, he had been a decent enough looking kid, yet not overly handsome. He did seem to lack that 'pretty boy' look all the girls were dreamy about, but still, he didn't lack for much since he did see his fair share of giggling girls and their flirtatious 'forget-me-not' looks.

As the years came and went and school was replaced by what became a lifelong career, Tandon made the transformation from the awkward boy of puberty to the full grown man. Many of the necessities of his job had required much physical strength and an overabundance of energy, and because of all that rigorous activity his physique had gradually been molded and sculpted into something even he was quietly impressed with. Even after he had retired, he had managed to maintain his strength and stamina. If it had decreased at all it was only slight and only what one would expect of someone at his age. Unfortunately though, these last months have taken their toll on him. His reflection, magnified in the truck's mirror, was proof enough of that. Tandon was careful to watch the road as he studied himself in the raw light of the day.

The cancer that had been ravaging him for

The Chimney Still Stands

years had caused a metamorphic change to occur. The tinted prescription glasses he had needed the past ten years just barely concealed the dark, blotchy area enveloping his eyes. His thick brown hair had turned a thin, dull gray and had receded far enough to be nearly extinct. Worse yet, his skin wasn't the deep and healthy tan it once was. A rough and rugged look had once boasted a proud and solid character, but now, thin and sallow, he resembled only a mock replica, an old washed out version of his former self. More than a little dejected, he groaned, cursing himself for not having readjusted the mirror when he'd had the chance.

* * *

In his preoccupation, Tandon had driven further down the mountain than he had intended and now he had to find somewhere to turn around. It seemed unlikely, though, since the old farm roads that had cut through these woods thirty years ago were now completely masked over with new growth.

Tandon had no choice except to continue on until he reached the river. When he finally did, he pulled into one of the many available parking spaces intent on turning around, but decided he'd relax and look around for a moment first.

What he saw really wasn't that surprising. In fact, he had fully expected it, but it still made him feel uncomfortable nonetheless. The house, barns, and fences that he knew had once stood there, had all been torn down and replaced with a large campground and canoe access. The only building there now housed the public restrooms.

A gust of wind blew against the side of his car,

rocking it gently. His window was open a crack and he could feel the crispness of the air seeping in, drawing him closer, like a magnet, to breathe deeply of it. It wasn't enough - only a sample - enough to tease a thirsty man. He needed more.

Without looking, his hand found the knob and he began cranking the window open until it stopped. Tandon closed his eyes as he inhaled, his nostrils flaring, then exhaled, slowly, enjoying the coldness, the freshness, the pureness that only comes at this time of year. At this river.

With his head tipped back against the headrest, a peaceful lull crept over him. Only the sound of the water lapping against the rocks could be heard. Everything else was quiet.

* * *

As Tandon drifted off, his thoughts turned from one of peace to agitation. It had been two years since his doctor had looked at him with sympathy and announced, "You have prostate cancer." Despite surgery and radiation, the cancer had spread to his bones. Only medications and blood transfusions could ease his suffering and lengthen his days. But that allowance would only last so long.

Three weeks ago, after another battery of tests, Tandon heard the numbing results. He was dying. They couldn't say exactly how long he had, but they did know it would be soon.

Tandon had a decision to make and only one week ago, after torturous hours of debate, he made his final decision. He was going back. His time was nearing and he wanted it to be peaceful. Thirty-five years was too long to have fought the war raging within him. He could feel it now, that familiar acid, burning and rising within him. A taste of self-loathing and disgust over what he had done. A poisonous vomit he longed to retch up and finally be rid of but which always remained, churning inside, eating at him until at times he felt he would explode.

As he had done so many times throughout the years, Tandon struggled to push those burdensome feelings aside, grateful for the excuse to do so, but he was mindful that it was only temporary. It was something he needed and wanted desperately to come to terms with. It was why he was here after all… to face his demons.

With renewed purpose in mind, Tandon turned his truck around and headed back up the road; the tires spinning, complaining in the loose dirt, the engine straining against the steep incline. As he came around a bend and the road leveled off a bit he knew instinctively that this was it. He crept along slowly, his forearm resting on the door, his face leaning, peering across the road, his gaze burrowing into the forest.

A car came down the road heading toward the river and the couple inside waved as they passed by. Tandon returned the wave distractedly, continuing his search.

He was nearing the next bend when something caught his attention and immediately he stopped the truck. He stared hard, squinting to see through the trees, blinked, and stared again. "Well, I'll be," he said, an odd mixture of excitement and tension coming over him.

Confident that his mind wasn't playing tricks on him and sure that he was seeing what he was seeing, he pulled the truck off the road, shut off the engine, and stepped out. The road that had once existed here was now overrun with tall grass and brush. The average passer-by would not have known that this had once been a private drive, but for Tandon the rusted chain he saw a few yards in was confirmation enough.

After gathering his belongings, Tandon walked in the few yards and lifted the heavy chain into his age-spotted hands. He stared blankly at it while his mind took him beyond the road block, the overgrown drive, and back to the past. Back to the questions he had once asked himself. Questions that had challenged his loyalty, faith, and integrity.

With a slight shake of his head, his pensive gaze focused again on the chain. He knew why it was there, what it meant. It was to keep the public out. But he wasn't the public. He wasn't just anyone. He was the one who had put the chain there.

Raising the chain Tandon ducked and stepped forward beneath the barrier, helpless to stop himself, and with a heavy heart and nervous step, began the journey back.

CHAPTER ONE

SPRING 1970

"Gentlemen, let's start the meeting please."

All conversation ceased while feet shuffled and rollers screeched into position as plush chairs succumbed under the weight of their occupants, all of whom promptly directed their attention to Greg Zimmerman, director of the National Park Service in Washington, D.C.

"Thank you," Greg began. "I am sure you have all heard about the proposal to include the Buffalo River in northwest Arkansas into the 'system'?" Nods of agreement went around the room.

Greg picked up the files that lay before him and stretched out his arm to drop them with a loud smack onto the center of the table. Everyone reached out to take one as Greg continued.

"Congress is requesting a second survey of the proposed ninety-five thousand acres. This had been done once before in '61 and the Senate passed their bill last year based on that previous survey. But before the House hearing begins, which is scheduled for late next year, they want an updated evaluation.

"Now we know there is a problem with the landowners along the river. These farmers...these families stand to lose homes, crops, grazing land, and the income that land has provided for them. Many of these families have inherited their land down the line beginning with their ancestors who first settled there. So you can see where their determination to keep their land is coming from." The men around the table again nodded in agreement.

"As of today, there are no national rivers in this country and the idea of having one, the Buffalo River in particular, is favored by the majority of the people. Those against it make up a rather small minority and though our intentions are to bring about positive results, we don't want to create dissension in the process."

Greg pushed back his chair and stood up, looking at each person in turn as he continued. "Now it has occurred to me that while we're documenting this survey, we could take this opportunity to make it clear to these landowners exactly where we stand and explain to them what will happen should the bills be passed. Hopefully we can change their minds, and if not, at least make them understand that we have their best interests in mind. And for that we need just the right voice."

As if sensing it would be one of them, the

surveyors turned to look at one another trying to guess who it might be before the director enlightened them.

"We have here among us the perfect man for the job. A man who has the distinct advantage of having been born and raised there," Greg stopped his roaming gaze to pin it squarely on the unsuspecting individual opposite him, "Tandon Bowman."

* * *

Tandon lay in his hotel bed, staring up at the stains in the ceiling, his fingers laced together cupping the back of his head, his thoughts a live firework display, despite the fact that he was physically exhausted and hadn't slept for what seemed an eternity.

Slowly Tandon pulled himself up to sit, shoulders slumped, on the edge of the bed. He turned his head to look at the clock and sighed. Only five-thirty. He stood and stretched before collecting some well-worn clothes on his way to the shower. Standing under the hot spray with his arms folded across his chest, his eyes closed, the memories of that fateful day, one month ago, returned.

The minute Greg Zimmerman had said his name it was as though a cannon-ball had found its mark in his stomach and it'd been lodged there ever since. He should have seen it coming, but foolishly didn't. He was being promoted, he was told, to manager of his own team.

Greg had said it was because of Tandon's dedication and hard work. That he deserved it. But it was obvious to Tandon, and to the other members of the team as well it seemed, that he had been handpicked only because of the particular usefulness he could provide.

It wasn't that he doubted Greg's sincerity or that of the Park Services'. What had been said was true. He had dedicated the past sixteen years of his life to the preservation of various marvels within the country. He had been wanting this for a long time and had always, confidently, known it would happen. The only dissatisfaction was in the timing. It not only looked bad, but it felt bad too. If it were any other place he would have been assigned to he would have been ecstatic. But being sent back to the one place he had tried for so long to forget, and had for the most part been successful, until now, well he wasn't sure if he should look at this as a cruel joke or some kind of test. Either way he felt that he wouldn't fare well.

After four weeks of meetings with the team members he had chosen, making plans about where to survey, checking over the trucks, getting the equipment in order, and making the two day drive, now the real test would begin.

After forty-five minutes Tandon was dressed and ready to go. Putting the hotel key in his pocket, he headed out to the nearest diner.

* * *

Harrison, Arkansas was a small town, and therefore, one in which everyone knew everyone. Waiting for his coffee at his seat in a booth, Tandon heard conversation coming from every direction. Everyone trying, it seemed, to be heard above the feverish pitch. He couldn't help but overhear what all the ruckus was about.

"Yeah, they think they're going to send down some high almighty government swindler to try and change our minds."

"But Harvey, you were glad when they took our side to stand against those dams being built."

"Yeah, well I didn't count on 'em coming to steal our land right from under us. Swindling government..." The man named Harvey grumbled the rest of his thoughts under his breath.

There was another heated argument a few seats away.

"Why, you know they'll give you what your land is worth. I don't see what the problem is. I bet they'll even build you a new house if you make a big enough stink about it," said one young man to another.

"What do you know about it? You don't even own your own land," came the tart reply.

"You only come by it from your daddy when he died and left it to you. You didn't work on it yourself and earn it."

"What's that got to do with anything? I inherited it and it's enough to earn a living and start a family with. What have you got? Nothing! A pitiful little apartment and a job bagging groceries. You have nothing worth losing to worry about, so what do you care," and with that he got up and stomped out.

The conversations continued as Tandon ordered, ate, and listened while growing increasingly uncomfortable. He realized he was getting a taste of the local dissension he had read about in the files and knew he would encounter. It appeared, though, that the tension was tauter than he had anticipated.

Checking the bill and counting out his money he placed a tip on the table. As he scooted to the edge of the seat, he caught the attention of one of the older men in the next booth.

"Say stranger, what do you think of all this? You must have heard what everyone has been talking about. What do you think of the government taking away folks' land so they can protect a river that nobody's even hurting?"

Taken aback, Tandon was initially at a loss for words. Then, realizing that a problem lay just ahead, he opted to save his opinions for the meeting later that evening. "I would really like to join you men in your discussion, but I reckon if you'll be attending the meeting tonight in Jasper you can hear from me then." With a nod he stood and walked out of the diner.

Tandon got into his truck and started the engine. Taking a deep breath, he realized that what he had anticipated from the town's folks would be all that and more, and it would only worsen when they found out who he was. The nagging sense of doom he had felt at getting this job was there again, staring him in the face. He had a gut feeling that this whole situation marked the beginning of something akin to hell for himself.

Looking down, Tandon saw the gas gauge was almost on empty, so he pulled into the nearest station. Intending to fill her up, he locked the nozzle and went inside for a drink. While he waited he walked over to the newspaper rack. As he fished in his pocket for change he glanced at the "Newton County Informer". The headline jumped out, National Park Service To Hold Meeting!

Dropping in his change, Tandon opened the door and pulled out the paper. He paid for the gas and a Dr. Pepper thanking the cashier, the bell chimed as he opened the door to leave. Glancing at the paper as he walked back to his truck something on the page caught his attention and he stopped suddenly. At the top was the name JulieAnn Peterson with the title 'Editor' printed beneath it.

Someone honked their car horn loudly, startling him. Waving distractedly he moved to his truck and got in, throwing the paper onto the seat beside him, and drove back to the hotel he was staying at. He nearly ran into his room, slamming the door behind himself. Flopping himself down on the bed, he spread open the paper and focused on her name. JulieAnn Peterson. His heart hammered against his chest.

As he stared at her name he saw her face in his mind. She was only seventeen the last time he had seen her. That was at his mother's funeral. It had only been one year earlier than that when they had been high school sweethearts. She was the prettiest girl in school with her long auburn hair and sky blue eyes. It was a striking combination. What was truly striking, though, was her genuine friendliness to anyone and everyone she met. No one was a stranger to JulieAnn.

He had always thought himself lucky that it

was he that she wanted to date. But it all came to an end a week after his graduation. The next time he heard from her was a year later to tell him his mother had died.

Knowing he had to focus on the job at hand Tandon pulled his thoughts together and read the short paragraphs concerning the time and location of the meeting to be held that night. Six p.m. Monday evening at the county courthouse in Jasper. Police would be there should a problem arise. There was no mention of whom the speaker would be and he presumed no one knew.

Tandon reached over to the bedside table to retrieve his folder. Knowing the discussion would become heated in the meeting, he decided he had better take another look over his file and make sure he was prepared for anything out of the ordinary.

* * *

There was a tinkling of the bells as the door opened. Rebecca Thomas let out a troubled sigh as she stopped and looked pleadingly at JulieAnn, her words coming out in a rush. "JulieAnn, I am so sorry. My son has the flu and I have no one to leave him with. I know I am supposed to be at the meeting tonight, but I just won't be able to. Do you think you can fill in for me? I hate to have to do this to you."

JulieAnn smiled sweetly at her friend. "Don't look so worried Becca. Of course I can. It's no problem at all." Concerned, she asked, "Is there anything I can help with? Do you need anything for Daniel?"

"No, no. Thanks. You're such a dear," she said

relieved and leaned over to give JulieAnn a big hug. "Is there anything you need me to work on while I'm at home?"

"No, hun. You just go and take care of that little man. And here," she said, reaching for the teddy bear she had gotten for him just that morning, "give this to him for me would you? Maybe that'll help him feel better." Smiling, she waved her friend off.

JulieAnn looked up at the clock, then checked it against the time on her watch. She had an hour until the meeting and decided she could quit what she was working on and pack her bag with her usual news paraphernalia. She grabbed her notebook and two good pens. You never want to run out of ink while the news is happening. She also grabbed her tape recorder and checked the batteries, remembering to bring extras. She'd learned her lesson at her last interview when her batteries had quit and she left having not recorded the second half of the meeting, only getting what she had managed to print on her notepad. Last of all was her camera. She especially enjoyed that part of her job, not to mention the fact that, through the years, it had become a sort of hobby that she delighted in every chance she had.

Finished with that she sat down at her desk. There was nothing left to do there and she didn't have any errands to run. There were no more excuses to use, no more reasons to keep up the struggle and she felt her resolve weaken for thoughts of the one man she had been trying hard to ignore all day.

Two years before he left, JulieAnn had known and understood Tandon's dream of working for the National Park Service. In fact, they'd had many talks about it. He had a flagrant passion for history and although she often giggled at his romanticizing of the stories he told her, she knew the day would come when those famous places he had only read about or seen in movies would steal him away.

It was the suddenness of his leaving that had surprised and hurt her. The fact that he had left without saying goodbye, and without letting her know where he was going, troubled and confused her. She had an idea of where he had gone, but was afraid to contact him out of fear that if he hadn't thought as much about their relationship as she had, she would make a fool of herself.

JulieAnn had done her best to push Tandon out of her mind. Then, late the next year, his mother had died. She had gone with her parents to offer her condolences and when her father asked Mr. Bowman if they could do anything, she unintentionally blurted out that she would find Tandon and let him know.

She had…and he came. Two days later, fighting back her own tears, she looked on as her old love mourned the loss of his mother. Afterwards, she would speak with him briefly, but only in the manner typical at funerals.

A few days ago, as she was putting the final touches to the NPS meeting announcement for the paper, she couldn't help wondering, hoping, that he might be with the team conducting the survey, and that he might come see her. "No. That's ridiculous," she had told herself getting to her feet. "Of all the places he could be working at, what are the chances he would end up here?" Then she added, sighing, "Especially since there's nothing here he wants."

Feeling the familiar pang of self-pity creeping alongside her thoughts, JulieAnn brought herself back to reality with a harsh scolding, "Stop it!" she said aloud. "Why do I do this to myself? I know better than this," she sighed, shaking her head, more than slightly annoyed with herself. She knew she should be getting over him by now. Should have a long time ago. But she couldn't. She didn't know why, really. She just couldn't.

JulieAnn grabbed her bag and walked to the door. As she flipped off the light switch she pushed away all thoughts of Tandon, setting her mind for the business at hand, and shut the door.

CHAPTER TWO

Tandon had decided it would be best if he arrived at the courthouse ahead of the town folk. It was a two story, gray stone, building set in the center of town with four roads bordering it and different businesses bordering them. It was typical of any small town square, but a bit of a culture shock for someone used to being in Washington, D.C.

Tandon walked up the stairs to the second floor and opened the door to the only courtroom in the building. It was a small room, he noted with mild surprise, considering the large crowd he was expecting, but he figured people would be willing to stand heel to toe for a meeting such as this. They had little choice since this was the only meeting place that could hold such a number of people at once. Unless they held it out on the lawn, he chuckled to himself. His humor dissipated somewhat when he realized that there was a good possibility of that happening. With a shrug, he walked forward to the front of the room.

Hanging on the wall, high above the bench, was a large portrait of the first judge that ever presided in that court room. To the left was the door to the judge's chambers. The name above the door read, "Judge Skinner". Tandon opened the door and stepped inside. It was a small room with a decent sized, hand carved, oak desk with a leather recliner behind it. Legal books lined the shelves of a bookcase that covered one whole wall.

Tandon stepped up to the desk and set his bag on it. As he did so, he took a look out of the window that was directly behind the desk. He watched as the vehicles began lining up and down the narrow road and knew it would be the same on the other three sides of the square. What vehicles were not already parked were making their way slowly onto side streets searching for any available spot. People were gathering around in groups talking, and he could feel the excitement mounting even from where he stood on the second floor.

Taking a deep breath, he turned around and pulled out his NPS folder with all of his notes for his referral during the meeting. Flipping it open for a quick review he paced the room. Coming to a stop at the door, he heard the hushed voices of two of the officers that would be chaperoning the meeting, obviously oblivious to the ears burning on the other side of the door.

"I don't know if anything is going to happen tonight, but I am thinking if anyone starts going after this guy," the voice lowered to a conspiring whisper, "I may just forget I wear a badge."

"Mmm, I hear ya," said his partner. "How

much land will you lose if this bill passes?"

"One hundred acres. Even if they bought it from me it would never equal the amount I would have made if I stayed and worked it," he said as they walked off.

Tandon shook his head and sighed. Everyone thinks the NPS is against them. He wished they understood it was just the opposite.

* * *

The courtroom was booming with activity and voices. The townsfolk had been filing in for half an hour. It sounded like the whole town and even the surrounding towns had shown up. Tandon pictured in his mind the old western movies where the people crowded around the center of town to watch the hanging of someone who had dared break the trust of the people. It sent a slight shiver down his back.

Tandon stared at the large clock on the wall, wondering if there was any speculation as to his whereabouts. He hadn't made mention that he was already there. They probably assumed he would come in after everyone else. They probably even figured he would be late, but tardiness had never been a problem for him. He was a born perfectionist priding himself on his promptness.

At six o'clock, on the dot, Tandon turned the door knob and stepped out of the judge's chambers. As he did so he focused on the two officers that stood ready at either side of the bench behind the podium he would be speaking from. He paused at the door and looked them directly in the eyes. The two officers, realizing that Tandon must have been in there at the time they spoke of him, grew hot under their collars and they both looked down at their feet like young children caught with their hand in the cookie jar.

The air was so thick and stuffy with the heat of all those bodies crammed into the small room, and the noise volume so high, that no one seemed to notice as he stepped to the front of the room and placed his NPS folder onto the podium. Then gradually, heads turned, recognized his brown Park Service uniform, and spread the word that the "enemy" was there.

While everyone seated themselves Tandon grew uncomfortable as those who recognized him began to lean over in their seats to spread that shocking news to their neighbor. It was like watching fans at a baseball game doing the wave, though it was clear, from the looks he was receiving, that these were not fans. Tandon felt both a chill and a suffocating heat as disdainful looks were turned his way.

* * *

JulieAnn could not believe who she was seeing. After all these years. After all her vain attempts to forget him. Now, there he was, standing right in front of her. And all she could do was stare at him.

As she did, she was overcome by how much he had changed. His features were similar of course, but more hardened than they were years ago. Physically he was more sculpted too, something his drab uniform failed to hide. This sinewy man before her was quite a contrast from the lanky boy she once knew and she found it impossible to tear her gaze away.

During these same moments she heard, as if from a distance, the whispers, his name spoken from their stiffened lips and heard the contemptuous tones in their voices as word spread of who he was. But to JulieAnn none of that mattered. What did, was the fact that he was back. He was finally back.

* * *

Tandon watched the ripple course around the room until, finally, it reached its conclusion, with his eyes coming to rest upon a familiar face. As he watched, the woman took a deep, shuddering breath, and it was then, with a sudden jolt of awareness, that he recognized her. She was staring right at him, her blue eyes sparkling like glass from the moisture that dampened them. Helplessly, he returned her stare.

JulieAnn, Tandon saw, was even more breathtaking than he remembered. Her once glorious, long, straight hair was now a sleek and soft shoulder length cut. A style which, surprisingly, had the effect of making her appear angelic. She was dressed casually in jeans and a simple v-neck tee shirt that reminded him of years past, while her features and womanly curves brought a new sense of maturity and beauty that he found intoxicating.

Tandon could have easily lost himself in the moment, as surprising to him as it was, but for the heavy strain he felt emanating through the room. Breaking their eye contact took some effort, but with a blink and a deep breath, and one last lingering look, he tore his gaze from hers.

Tandon looked down at his notes knowing he

needed to refocus on them and the task at hand. It took a concentrated effort, a determined force of willpower, to steer his mind back to his work. And after some successful, but agonizing moments, and a renewed sense of purpose for the evening firmly in place, Tandon calmly and suggestively cleared his throat into the microphone, looking on as the town folk quieted down and settled into their seats.

In a businesslike tone Tandon ordered, "Let's begin the meeting," and immediately heard pens click and pads flip open, including JulieAnn's he noted from the corner of his eye. "Let me first introduce myself for anyone who doesn't already know," he said, not missing the irony. "My name is Tandon Bowman. I am originally from Newton County, Arkansas...specifically here in Jasper, so some of us may be familiar with one another."

"So they sent you thinking if we knew you that we might be persuaded to change our minds. Well, think again!" a man yelled out earning sympathy from equally disgruntled peers.

Tandon expected to hear comments along those lines. Heck, he even thought it himself, so he couldn't really blame them for thinking it.

Tandon held up both hands, "Let's start this off on the right foot by letting me explain the purpose of this meeting. Congress has asked the National Park Service for a second survey of the ninety-five thousand acres they propose to buy. They hope this updated survey will reinforce the necessity of having the Buffalo River included into the Park Service system." Tandon took a steadying breath. "I am speaking with you tonight in the hope of dispelling any fears and misunderstandings by answering all of your questions and giving you all of the information you need."

Tandon relaxed his shoulders and spoke in a more familiar tone, wanting to reassure them somehow. "I want you to know that I have worked for the National Park Service for all of my adult life and in that time I have seen a loyalty and dedication to all causes of this kind. The NPS is not a government agency out for herself. We simply want to keep the memories and history alive, and in this case and many others, offer its protection for natural wonders."

A man in the back, whom Tandon recognized as the one who had questioned him at the restaurant, snorted and said, "Protection from what? This river was just fine until you government people started butting in, wanting to change it."

Tandon was glad he had prepared for such a comment. "This river is no longer safe from change and even I am sorry to say that." He received many bitter looks in response. "We came into the picture when it was brought to our attention that two dams were being proposed. We didn't see the logic in that and thought it would be better suited to us."

A frail looking woman stood up with some help from the younger man seated beside her and said in a thin, cracked voice, "Maybe I am a bit old fashioned sir, but I don't understand why we can't just let the river be as it has always been." Again, sympathy nods and gestures swept the room.

Tandon smiled politely, "You are not old fashioned ma'am. Your question is a valid one and I am very sympathetic to your feelings on this, to everyone's, but it's not that simple. Once the idea was brought up, the tide began to flow. You will always have different people with different ideas and that will never stop unless someone wins...so to speak."

A man stood up and introduced himself, "My name is Bob Thornton. I am the chairman of the Buffalo River Landowners Association." Tandon nodded and the man continued. "I heard you say the amount of land the NPS would acquire, should this get passed of course, would be ninety-five thousand acres. Is that correct?"

"Yes, that is correct," Tandon said.

"I think I can ask the question then that is on everyone's mind." Tandon knew what he was going to ask and was ready. He nodded to the man. "How many folks are going to have to lose their homes?"

Grasping the edges of the podium he replied, "Well, right now that is difficult to say. It is up to Congress to authorize land buying boundaries. When that is decided professional appraisers evaluate your land and then begins the land acquisition, the process, of acquiring that land."

"How much of that money are we going to be gypped of?" another asked.

"Sir, we have no intention of gypping you of anything. What you get will be a fair amount," to his surprise, the group began laughing. Tandon interrupted them. "Some of you will have choices. One, you can take the money and move to another location. Two, the government will buy your property and you can live there for twenty-five years. You also have the option of the life estate which simply means you may stay until the time of your death. Depending on your particular circumstances, Congress has a number of options.

"Are there any questions?" Tandon asked.

A woman stood up, "If this bill gets passed, how soon will we have to move out if that is what we choose?"

"It will take a few years to get to everyone living on the allotted land so it is really difficult to say who will be first and so on. You will need to wait to get word from them specifically.

"On another note," Tandon said, his tone serious, "from the moment the bill gets passed, the purchase price of your land is final. Should you think to add on any additions to your property, assuming you will receive a refund, then you should rethink that idea. You won't get anything over its worth at that time." It was clear to Tandon from some of the looks of the younger men that he had thwarted some plans. He gave them a direct look to bring home his point.

Tandon looked down at the last important note in his file and cleared his throat loudly to regain the people's attention. "We have one last thing to discuss before we bring this meeting to a close. It has come to our attention, in D.C., of some threats that have been made to blow up the bluffs and poison the trees the very minute the bill gets passed. I cannot imagine this type of 'revenge' as being very productive. All that would serve to do is kill the wildlife. Not to mention possibly killing an innocent bystander."

Tandon, exasperated that he should have to be discussing such a thing, shook his head, dumbfounded. "What is amazing to me, especially, is why you would ruin the exact things you claim to love about this area." He looked at the faces and shook his head again. "The theory that 'if I can't have it, no one will' is a foolish one. All you will gain from that is prison time and a very costly penalty.

"Now it would seem to me, from how willing you are to fight for this river that you would want to keep what you love intact. Please, think before you do something rash." Tandon closed his file and added, "I have workers all along the river area so the surveying shouldn't take too long. I'll be here for the week if you have any questions." And with that the meeting was adjourned.

* * *

Tandon was closing his briefcase, having double checked to make sure he had all of his notes. He knew he did, but he was fidgety. After the meeting he had come back into the judge's chambers wanting only to collect his things, but it had ended with him spending the last half hour sitting in the judge's chair. He had felt drained when it was all over and there was little relief from the tension he felt. Deciding he had wasted enough time, he grabbed the handle of his briefcase and headed to the door.

As Tandon exited the building and headed for his truck he noticed JulieAnn sitting on a bench. As he neared, she stood up and waited as he closed the distance between them. They looked at each other for a long moment before JulieAnn said haltingly, "I just want to know if you have anything you would like to add for the paper?"

Once again, Tandon couldn't seem to get his eyes off of her. "No," he said, "I think I said everything."

There was another awkward pause before they said in unison, "How are you?" and laughed, relieving some of the tension.

Tandon let her answer first, "I'm good," she said. "I'm the editor of the paper now," Tandon managed to look as amazed as he had when he saw her name in the newspaper, "And you?" she asked.

"I'm good," he mimicked. "I'm the manager of a National Park Service team." Tandon could have kicked himself when he realized how ridiculous that sounded.

There was a long uncomfortable silence as Tandon searched for something to say. He looked at his watch and said, "It's late. Have you eaten yet? If you haven't we can go grab something."

"Actually, I have and it is late. I was going home to start on the article," she said, her hands busy fidgeting with the straps of the bag she held tightly before her.

Tandon worried for a moment. He really wanted to see her again. Suddenly he felt hope. "Would you like to meet for lunch tomorrow? Anywhere you like," he said eagerly.

He saw her dimple as she grinned, "Okay. I'll call you tomorrow. Where are..."

"At the Holiday Inn," he interrupted.

JulieAnn nodded and smiled at him. "Well,

good night then."

"Good night," Tandon smiled back and watched her turn and walk to her car. As she drove away, she looked one last time and Tandon held his hand up to her.

CHAPTER THREE

Tandon woke Tuesday morning feeling refreshed and invigorated having finally gotten a good night's rest, even earning himself a few extra hours to make up the difference.

The phone was ringing as Tandon shut off the water to the shower. He had a feeling it would be JulieAnn, so wrapping a towel around himself, he scurried to the bedside and picked up the receiver. "Hello," he said pleasantly.

There was silence at the other end, then a man's voice, "Tandon?"

Tandon stifled a sigh, "Yes, this is he." Hearing nothing he said, "Can I help you?"

In a voice that was barely audible the speaker said, "I am not surprised you don't recognize my voice. You haven't bothered with me in fifteen years."

Tandon was surprised by the sudden darkness that came over him. "Father." The word tasted like dirt in his mouth.

"How typical that I should hear about your visit from Butch."

Tandon recalled his father's longtime friend. "I thought I would see you at the meeting last night," he said tightly.

Disregarding that his father continued, "Come out here today. We have something to discuss," he said and abruptly hung up.

Tandon slammed the receiver back onto its base then stood up suddenly and grabbed his shirt, punching his fists into the sleeves. His father hadn't changed a bit. Still ordering him around, even after all this time. He slammed his feet into his jeans. What infuriated him most was that he had already planned to stop by and see him, but now, because his father had made the first move, it made him look like he was a thoughtless child again. He stomped his foot into his boot, yanking the laces tight. Well, he'd go this time, but if his father thinks he's going to kowtow to him, well then, he has another thing coming.

The phone rang again and Tandon answered abruptly, "Yeah?" and was immediately sorry when he heard the delicate voice.

"Tandon? Hi, it's JulieAnn."

"Hi. I am sorry about that. I just got off the phone," he said.

She dismissed that without comment. "I just wanted to call and tell you I would like to have lunch if you still want to," she said.

Tandon felt better already. Smiling he said, "I do. Did you decide where you would like to go?"

"No. I'll leave that up to you. You can pick me up at the office around noon though."

"That sounds fine. I have a couple errands to run this morning first but I'll be there at noon."

"I'll see you then."

Tandon could hear the smile in her voice. "See you then," he returned and hung up.

Knowing he wasn't going to get any work done today, he promised himself he would make up for it tomorrow, but before he went to see his father he had something more personal to do first.

* * *

Tandon turned off the highway and drove two miles of dusty road until he saw the small enclosure. The sign hanging above the gate read, "Pine Cemetery". He parked the car and walked in to where his mother's marker was. There were flowers there, but they had long since died and withered. Tandon assumed his father had put them there and vaguely wondered when the last time was that he had been out there.

Wanting to make his own contribution he looked around and spotted some wild flowers growing outside the fence. He walked over and picked some and brought them back to his mother's grave. He read the headstone.

Martha Bowman

1912-1952

Beloved mother and wife

Friend to all

Tandon remembered how beautiful she was. He was always so proud when she came to school functions. Some of the other kids pretended they didn't know their parents, but he was always happy when she was there. When he would wave to her, the other kids would follow suit and yell, "Hi mom," which would always make her laugh.

She was diagnosed with having breast cancer when he was seventeen. They found it late and they said she only had a couple of months to live. It tore him apart and she knew it. He remembered the talk they had one night as she lay bedridden.

He had looked into her pale blue eyes, "Tandon," she said, holding his hands, "you know that I won't be here much longer." She squeezed his hand slightly as the tears formed in his eyes. "You need to know how proud I am of you. All I ever wanted was to have a family. I prayed about it every day. And here you are," she said, a smile creasing her face, "the answer to all my prayers. From the moment you were born, I have watched you and listened to you and even learned from you. And what I have seen is enough to comfort me and give me peace. I couldn't be more proud of you."

Tandon wiped his arm across his face, unable to stop the flow of tears, "I'm proud of you too, maw," he gulped.

His mother smiled back, her own eyes glistening with tears. Suddenly squeezing his hand with a strength he hadn't seen in a while, her voice stronger too, she said, "Now...I know you and your father have been having some problems. I want you to forget about them. Being angry is no way to live your life. I know your father is a hard man to get along with, but you have to find that place within yourself that can get past what he is and just love him for who he is."

He wasn't sure he could do that, but when he saw his mother slump in weakness he realized just how important it was to her. "You're right maw, I'll try," he had said, but it wasn't to be. The very next day he and his father had fought. His father wanted him to work the farm full time now that he was out of school, but Tandon had other ideas and they didn't include home. He wanted to go work for the National Park Service.

As usual, the fight solved nothing, instead only made it worse. Tandon decided that it would be best if he left. His heart wasn't there anymore. The only thing he would regret would be leaving his mother while she was still sick.

"Maw," he said when he went into her room that evening. "I can't stay here. I'm sorry, but being a farmer isn't what I'm cut out for," he said passionately. "I want to see the country. I love it here, this is the only place I know, but I need more."

"I know son. I have always known you would leave."

Tandon began to cry, "I don't know what to do. I don't want to leave you," his head fell and his shoulders shook with emotion.

His mother put her hand under his chin and lifted until he looked at her. "Tandon, follow your heart. If it tells you that this is the moment to take charge of your life, then obey it. I have raised you to know your own mind and make your own decisions. Now you can show me how well I did." She smiled, "Go on now. Don't worry about me. I'm in the best hands."

The Chimney Still Stands

Tandon's tears had stopped as he listened to his mother. How strong she was. He had always known it, but right then, he really admired her. "I will make you proud of me. I promise." Tandon leaned over and kissed her cool cheek. "I love you maw," he said and walked to the door.

When he turned back, she whispered, "I love you son," as a tear slid down her cheek.

Tandon bent down on one knee and set the flowers down gently. He didn't know what to say. He didn't think she would be very proud of him now. He and his father never patched things up and now here he was, working to take land and homes from her friends. He wasn't sure what she would say if she were here now, but he sure could have used her advice.

Tandon stood up and said simply, "I miss you maw," and turned back to his truck.

* * *

"Hey Jul's, got any charcoal outback?" Jess asked, walking in unannounced letting the screen door shut behind him.

JulieAnn grinned looking up, pleasantly distracted from the bills she had been looking over at the kitchen table knowing full well that just the other day her brother had seen her at the grocery store buying charcoal to grill some hamburgers.

"Nope," she answered sweetly watching as her brother took his usual route to the refrigerator for something cold and bubbly.

"No?" he asked quizzically unsure whether she was teasing him or not. He turned around pulling a Coke out from the refrigerator, walked over to the counter and popped the bottle cap off.

She could not help but laugh at the funny look on his face. "Of course. There's two bags on the back porch. Help yourself."

Jess stuck his tongue out at her playfully and headed off toward the back porch. "You going to the game tonight sis? We're going to have a barbecue after."

Normally JulieAnn went to her brother's baseball games unless an article needed to be finished for publication, but on the whole, she tried to make it a point of supporting her brother in as many games as she possibly could. However, after a pause, she answered, "I think so."

"You think so?" Jess chuckled. "What else are you going to do?"

"Well," she paused, not sure whether she should tell her brother or not. It was a sensitive subject and she knew it might cause a lot of problems. "I'm going out this afternoon is all and," she looked away, guilty, for a brief moment, "I'm not sure if I'll be back in time for your game."

"Where're you going?" Jess asked.

JulieAnn looked down at the table and shrugged her narrow shoulders. She didn't know what to say.

"Hey Jul's," Jess said with a little laugh, "Are you keeping a little secret from me? Is there something you want to tell me?"

With her back toward her brother she quirked an eyebrow and thought, "Yeah! And what a 'something' it is."

Jess had put the bags of charcoal down by the

door and walked back to the counter. In one smooth movement, he pulled himself up to sit on the counter top.

Squaring her shoulders and lifting her chin, JulieAnn announced, "I'm going on a date."

Jess' eyes widened in surprise as he waited expectantly for his sister to continue. "Well, who is he?" he pressed after only a moment.

JulieAnn looked her brother straight in the eye. "Tandon Bowman," she said, watching his eyes widen further in surprise.

"He's here?"

She nodded. "He was here last night at the meeting. He's directing the survey." JulieAnn watched as varying emotions crossed her brother's face.

Just short of two years separated their births and yet one would think they had been born twins. As children they were always together, sharing every experience, every memory. Their whole family was very close, but the two had formed a special bond. One was rarely seen without the other. It was like their own secret club. What one did the other knew. Their closeness had gotten them through many a situation together.

Jess was the first one who knew about her attraction to Tandon. The first she told when he finally got around to asking her out. And he was the first to know when the boy she had fallen head-over-heals in love with, left her. And it was that knowledge that Jess had about Tandon and herself that she saw passing over her brother's face.

JulieAnn had stopped talking about Tandon

long ago because it was too painful. When Tandon's mother died, and she had to contact him, a large part of her was hopeful that he would come back to stay. But when she did see him it seemed as though she was seeing, in him, an even stronger urge to escape than before. They had exchanged meaningful looks and small words, but little else before he was gone again.

After Tandon had left, JulieAnn had started going over to his father's place to clean his home. Freshen things up a bit. Bring him flowers. She knew everyone thought she was just trying to do the right thing, and that is what she wanted also, but yet, she knew more than that, that her motives were more selfish. She wanted to hear word of Tandon. What she did hear of him was never any good. His father and he did not get along. Whenever his father spoke of Tandon it was with bitterness. But his name alone was worth hearing.

Jess knew that she went over to Tandon's fathers to do these things for him, but the loneliness she felt was something she wanted to keep to herself. Not even that did she want to share with her brother, though she suspected he knew. Sometimes she felt Jess watching her very closely, such as when she returned from her visits. She knew he was trying to read her, but it was something she just could not give away. And to his credit, he never pushed. They were very loyal to each other and trusted each other's opinion, and that was why, she guessed, she did not want to talk about it with him. She needed to hang on to what she had left of Tandon.

"Jess?" JulieAnn asked, breaking the silence. She watched as her brother slid down from the counter, his face expressionless, and moved to take a seat at the table. He sat for only a moment before changing his mind, preferring instead to pace the floor.

Glancing at his sister in mid-stride he said, "I don't know what to say," and continued on, completing one full cycle around the room before coming to a standstill before her. "What do you want me to say?" he asked. "Hurray for you...Glad he's back...Now you can get on with the rest of your life?" Jess sighed, throwing his hands up. "Sis, you haven't heard from the guy in over a decade. And now he shows up, and for no other reason than to do his job mind you, and you're ready to jump into his arms."

Jess saw the tortured look on his sister's face and sighed again, "I'm sorry sis, but don't you remember what he did to you...his family? Not to mention the part he's playing now. JulieAnn, our own grand-mother's going to lose her home, and you want to date a guy who thinks that's okay. Who's encouraging it, in fact." Jess looked at her strangely, "What are you thinking?"

JulieAnn jumped up from her seat, making her brother take a step back. "Oh, for goodness sake, it's not really even a date. We're just going to talk. I'll find out how he's been and vice versa." Her impatience quickly fled as she looked sadly at her brother and said almost whispering, "I have to see him before he leaves. I may never see him again."

Jess looked at her, her eyes melting his heart,

and knew that no matter what he said, his sister would go through with it. He couldn't really blame her. In a way, he understood. He knew how much she still thought about him, still loved him. If the shoe were on the other foot, he knew he'd do the same. He just wished it was happening to him and not his sister. He just wished it wasn't happening…period.

JulieAnn watched her brother and could see the battle he was fighting wanting both to protect her and at the same time let her do what she needed to do. When she saw his expression soften she smiled encouragingly.

Jess gave in with a reluctant sigh, "I can see you have your mind set on this so I'll stand behind you." He couldn't help smiling at his sister's contagious grin.

JulieAnn moved to hug her brother and said, "Thanks, Jess." In just a short while she would see Tandon, and though a sensible part of her wanted to overshadow her happiness with caution, another part was hopeful and exhilarated. And so she stubbornly pushed it away as she looked up at her brother…beaming.

CHAPTER FOUR

The shaded road began to warm as the mid-morning sunlight filtered through the canopy of branches stretching high overhead. Birds and small, furry, critters scurried here and there amidst the thick, lush, foliage carpeting the forest on either side. Cautiously, Tandon eased his truck down the road, peering to the left, then the right, giving all attention to picking up the slightest movement of a head, the telltale twitch of an ear, a tail. Anything that would direct his gaze to the animal's camouflaged position.

Looking for deer amidst open fields and dense forests, even along roadsides, had been a habit since youth. It served as a great diversion from a stressful day, a long boring drive, or a cluttered mind. And today was no different. Today Tandon was seeking distraction from the storm to come. The 'battle of the wills' as someone had once called it. And it was getting closer with every rotation of the truck's wheels.

Unsuccessful in his search, Tandon gave up just as the forest came to an abrupt end and opened up instead to reveal a breathtaking view of sun drenched fields, rolling hills, and a colonnade of mountains. This view had always been a pleasant surprise to their family and friends that had come to visit. Even, on occasion, the unknown photographer had been found rearranging this and focusing that, seeking to capture that perfect Kodak moment. Tandon remembered one such gentlemen had, in fact, won first prize in an Arkansas nature magazine for his submission, "Utopia." He had sent his parents the picture and article which his mother had proudly framed. He wondered if it still hung in the living room.

Tandon steered his truck to the left where the house sat overlooking the view and parked outside of the fence, in the graveled area used just for that purpose, before stepping out. The house was a somewhat small, two-story, box with a white painted porch, two rocking chairs that he was surprised to see were still the same, and a potted plant on the table between. He recognized his childhood home, and yet he didn't. Maybe it was the size of it that surprised him - he had always imagined it larger. Or perhaps it was the weathered gray siding that stole the brightness from the gleaming white he remembered. And he was certain there had never been vines climbing alongside the house, nor up the chimney.

Oddly enough, these differences made him feel uncomfortable and somewhat out of place. Like a stranger. Well, truth be told, he was. Time has passed and a lot of things have changed in the last sixteen years. He is as different a person today as he was back then.

Tandon turned his head slightly, taking it all in, and caught his eye on the flowers coming in along the front of the house. A tender smile touched his lips. One thing hadn't changed. The daffodils his mother had planted were still going strong. He could almost see her there, bent over, lovingly planting each bulb. It was comforting to see evidence of her life blossoming, faithful and steadfast, through the years. He knew with certainty she would be pleased.

Breaking away from his thoughts, Tandon turned his attention to the fields, half of which had been used for grazing and the other for haying. From the looks of it, the former hadn't seen a herd in quite some time, but the latter showed signs of a new crop growing in with a few bales left along the tree line from the past winter lending proof to the previous season's success.

"They're going to take it all you know," his father said having walked up, noiselessly, behind him. Tandon stiffened and turned to face his father, saying nothing. Isaac Bowman nodded his head in the direction of the fields, "All the work I put into fixing this land. All the long hours. All that time and effort ...wasted," his father shook his head, his lip curled in disgust, "just so Uncle Sam can reach down with his almighty hand and snatch it away."
Father and son looked at each other for a moment in tense silence before Isaac turned, leaving Tandon to

follow suit. "Why did you come back?" Isaac asked over his shoulder.

"My team…" Tandon began.

"No," his father interrupted swinging around suddenly, "I want to know what you are doing here. Oh, don't get me wrong," he said, resuming his pace, "I knew you'd show up one day. I just figured it'd be at my funeral. That you'd come back to stab me in the back never occurred to me."

Ignoring his father's sarcasm, Tandon said, "Look, I didn't come here to fight with you. This is my job and these are the orders I was given, whether I liked it or not."

Isaac spun around, pouncing on his son's words, "If you didn't like it then why didn't you turn them down? Tell them you knew these people and that you could never do that to them"

"Do you think that would have mattered? That that would stop them? They would have just sent someone else." Tandon said shrugging his shoulders.

"And God forbid that should happen. I suppose the temptation to twist the knife was just too great." Isaac said, heading off again toward an old truck parked with its hood open. As though the thought just occurred to him, he added with a harsh laugh, "I wouldn't be surprised to know you were expecting a promotion when you got back."

Tandon's head snapped up surprised by how close his father was to the truth. He was sorely tempted to tell him he'd already been promoted, but thought better of it. Mainly because of his own guilt over what he believed were the reasons behind his promotion, but also because he didn't want to give his father further reason to patronize him.

"I don't know how you got it into your head that I'm to blame for all of this," Tandon said.
"You act as though I'm personally responsible for creating and carrying out this whole situation myself."

"I know better than that," his father scoffed.

"Do you? Then why are you being so hard on me?"

Isaac turned around to gesture to his house and fields, "Take a look around here. This is where you were born...where you grew up. I bought and worked this land, and built this home with my own two hands," he shook his outstretched hands, "for my family. Does that mean nothing to you?"

"Of course it does," Tandon said, realizing his father was straying from the subject of his business here and becoming more personal.

"Then why wasn't it good enough for you? Why did you leave your dying mother, and me, to cope alone? What was your rush?" Isaac was nearly yelling, "Come on. I want to know."

Frustration welled up in Tandon as he clenched his jaws, struggling to put into words the onslaught of emotions that threatened to overwhelm him. He had known that morning that the conversation between he and his father might lead to this, but he had stubbornly pushed it aside, having convinced himself it would stay on the subject of the work he was doing instead. He was a fool for not having been prepared. And disgusted with his father for having put him on the spot.

Fed up with his own stupidity, Tandon threw up his hands, "What's the point of going into this now. Just forget it," he said and turned away, heading toward his truck. "I should have known better than to come here. Nothing ever changes."

"That's right," his father yelled after him, "run away again."

Tandon swung around on his heel stomping a few feet toward his father. "That's right. I ran away. But if you want to know why, maybe you should ask the right question. Instead of, 'Why wasn't it good enough for me?' why don't you try, 'Why wasn't I good enough for you?'"

"What are you talking about?" his father asked frowning at him.

"Oh you remember don't you? Those little cat and mouse games you like to play with me. I tell you something, you thumb your nose at it and give me a better idea." Tandon looked at his father, unable to keep the smirk off his face, "It didn't matter how trivial or important it was, you'd manage one way or another to disintegrate my ideas and glorify yours all in the same breath."

"Your mother always said you were a dreamer. You were always coming up with impossible ideas. All I did was end your false hopes and give you goals you could reach."

"So long as they fell in line with what you had planned," Tandon said, "Even when I was young you could never just humor me. You were too busy one-upping me. But here we are now," Tandon said, raising his arms at his sides, "and it looks like one of my dreams came true."

"Yeah. And look what you're doing with it."

Tandon let his arms fall to his sides. "You know what," he sighed, shaking his head. "it's useless trying to talk to you. You turn everything into a contest. I'm tired of competing. You win. Have it your way."

Tandon turned away and a few steps later turned back, "Oh, by the way…about the river? Most of your state, in fact, most of your country, is in favor of nationalizing this river. It is a shame that some will lose their homes, sure, but you know what? It's going to happen. This is one battle you won't win," and with that Tandon swung around, finishing the distance to his truck, feeling his father's eyes burn into his back.

* * *

JulieAnn walked into the newspaper office to find Rebecca working on the printer. "Good morning," she said cheerfully as Rebecca looked up, "How's Daniel doing?"

"Oh, he's better. His fever broke last night, but he's still a little weak, so my mother is watching him today. Oh, by the way," she said coming around the machine and moving to her desk, "Daniel made you a picture of himself," Rebecca handed JulieAnn a slightly wrinkled piece of paper. "That's the teddy bear you gave him," she smiled, pointing to a brown colored shape in the little boy's hands. "He slept with it all night curled up in his arms. When I woke up this morning, he was sitting at his desk drawing this for you."

JulieAnn could see the pride in her friend's eyes as she talked about her son and she thought she understood. She would be proud too to have a husband who adored her and a son who could charm the pants off of anyone.

JulieAnn had known Rebecca for ten years now and although she had watched from the sidelines as her friend was courted by Collin, now her husband of eight years, and witnessed the birth of their first child, now six, she had never sunk to the degree of jealous envy that if allowed, could have ruined their friendship. Instead, JulieAnn had always been sincerely happy for her, knowing that when the time was right, she too would find her prayers answered.

Asking Rebecca to thank Daniel for her, JulieAnn taped the picture to the wall behind her desk as Rebecca walked back to the printer and asked, "How was the meeting last night?"

The innocent question brought a wistful look to JulieAnn, who sat softly in her chair immediately lost in thought, seeing Tandon's face in her mind, recalling the feelings that had assailed her only hours ago. The surprised jolt of her heart when she first saw him standing, unaware of her, at the podium. Her breath held as she memorized every expression…mannerism, every detail of his matured features. She felt again the inferno aroused in her veins as their eyes met, the force of his gaze drawing her in, making her forget that anyone else existed. She felt again the passions of her youth as she stood before him outside the courthouse. Saw the streetlights reflected in the luminous flecks of his hazel green eyes. The evidence of his sun kissed skin, darker in the shadows of the night. His dark hair, softly stirring in the balmy evening air. His rich, earthy voice…

"Ahem," Rebecca cleared her throat loudly waking JulieAnn from her daydreaming. JulieAnn blinked and looked up to find her friend standing in front of her desk with a humorous twinkle in her eye. "Pleasant dreams?" she asked with an inquisitive smile.

JulieAnn blushed, hoping her thoughts weren't as transparent as her face must have been. She feigned sudden interest in the articles on her desk, looking through, but not really seeing any of them before pausing, remembering Rebecca had asked her something, and looked up to inquire, "What did you ask me?"

Having never seen JulieAnn this way before, Rebecca was indeed enjoying every minute of her obvious discomfort. "The meeting?" she repeated.

"Right," she said, trying to act nonchalant about the whole thing. "It went well. He gave some details about what would happen when the bill was passed. He tackled a lot of questions and gave a few warnings. And afterwards I took down some statements from the residents. I thought tomorrow we could get started on the articles."

"Not today?" Rebecca asked surprised. Since this was such an important piece she just assumed they would start on it right away.

"No. I'll be going out this afternoon. I have a meeting with the manager of the team." Rebecca nodded her head, understanding. "You have to interview him."

JulieAnn stopped her fussing but kept her head down, "Well…no, actually. We're going to have lunch." She snuck a quick glance at Rebecca and saw her staring strangely at her. Taking a deep breath, she explained, "His name is Tandon Bowman and he grew up here." JulieAnn shrugged her shoulder and added, "We used to date."

Rebecca gasped, a wide smile spreading across her face. Despite their long friendship this was news to her, but she dismissed it as inconsequential. "You're kidding?" she said. When she could see she wasn't, Rebecca asked, "When was this?"

JulieAnn grinned, "In high school. We were together almost three years."

"Was it serious?" Rebecca asked.

JulieAnn nodded, "Yes. Or, at least I thought it was." Seeing Rebecca raise her eyebrows questioningly, JulieAnn added, "He left after graduation to work for NPS. We basically lost touch after that."

"Oh." Rebecca could sense the sadness behind JulieAnn's casual tone. "So…" she hesitated, "you're going to catch up on old times today?"

JulieAnn smiled in anticipation, "Yeah."

Rebecca saw a dreamy look coming over JulieAnn and hated to ask, but did so, "How long will he be here?"

JulieAnn's expression sobered slightly, "One week," she said, her eyes straying involuntarily to the calendar on her desk. "He leaves next Monday."

Rebecca didn't say anything. In the short amount of time they had been talking, JulieAnn had explained, verbally, but mostly non-verbally, the reasons behind her failed, would be, romances. In the years that she'd known JulieAnn, Rebecca had watched her date several men, even setting her up with one, but they never went any further than the second or third date. From what she had gathered there had never been anything wrong with any of them, and despite her own curiosity, JulieAnn never offered her reasons and she, not wanting to pry, never asked.

The bells jingled as the door to the office opened and both women looked up, distracted from their thoughts, to find a good looking man, wearing a pair of Levis, hiking boots, and a red checked flannel shirt that gave him the appearance of a lumberjack, stepping towards them, his mere presence shrinking the already small room.

The man gave Rebecca a polite smile, but instantly turned his attention to JulieAnn, who stood up slowly with an expression that said it all. Rebecca knew, without having to be told, that this was the man who favored JulieAnn's heart.

The man smiled at JulieAnn, "Hi."

JulieAnn returned both, "Hi."

CHAPTER FIVE

As Tandon and JulieAnn headed out of town and deeper into the countryside they talked, keeping the conversation light and casual, each offering the other a glimpse into the changes and challenges of the past years, each listening and rediscovering the other anew; both enjoying the ease with which the conversation was going, feeling comfortable and relaxed...as old friends would.

Tandon took JulieAnn back to the beginning, explaining how he had started his career by being a park ranger, first in Wyoming's Yellowstone Park, then being transferred to Bryce Canyon in Utah and later to Mammoth Cave in Kentucky. It was here, he explained, that he had gotten his first job as a guide, consequently needing to make his own request for a transfer, because as he smilingly put it, "I'd much rather walk on the ground than in it."

From there he had worked at National Military Parks such as Fort Donnelson in Tennessee,

The Chimney Still Stands

Horseshoe Bend in Alabama, and Vicksburg in Mississippi. Working in the military parks, he said, was his favorite, reminding her of his passion for old war stories, the Civil War in particular.

He described to her, in vivid detail, the imagery he saw as he stood in those old battle fields...envisioning the blinding smoke of the musketry, hearing the icy clanging of clashing swords and bayonets, and feeling the air and ground pulsating with every powerful blast of the cannons. He pictured the dead strewn out across the war ravaged expanse, heard the horrified cries of the wounded, and the anguished call of the dying soldier for his mother. In contrast, were the exhausted but victorious shouts of the avenged enemy, claiming triumph over death and allegiance to country.

It was a period in time that Tandon was inexplicably drawn to, and despite being born decades too late to have participated, he was grateful, he said, to have found a way to become involved with the honoring and preserving of the history he so loved.

Her own life, JulieAnn chuckled, was not so fascinating. After high school, she took a course in journalism in Fayetteville, driving many miles back and forth nearly every day for two years, meanwhile working part time at the paper until eventually graduating and soon after taking over as editor.

It was a good paper, she said humbly, but a small one filled with typical small town news. There were the annual holiday events such as the county festivals and parades. Summer activities were the usual fairs, rodeos, and church revivals. There were the weekly announcements from the citizens, businesses and charities, births, obituaries. And of course, there was always the local and state politics and stories of national interest. Their heaviest news, she said, occurred in these latest years over the Vietnam War, the local men serving, and their families.

JulieAnn also spoke about her family, knowing Tandon had always been fond of them. Her grandparents, Frank and Annabelle, while now in their late seventies, were still living well on their farmstead, although, they have put into retirement the fields and machinery and no longer have their four-legged food supply running around. Her parents, John and Sara, had bought the local feed store, and being the only one for miles around, were very successful.

Her eight younger brothers and sisters were also successful in their own right. Jess was the local mechanic who, through his job, had gotten together a group of locals to play baseball every spring. She added that tonight, in fact, they were playing a game. He was welcome to come. Two of her sisters were married, both to their high school sweethearts. Katie is a stay at home mother of three boys, and Marie, childless at the moment, is a nurse at the local hospital. Jack, Thomas, and Billy were flying through high school. Little Anna, named after their grandmother, was finishing up the eighth grade with the baby of the family, John Jr., ending his sixth year with an honor roll.

Tandon, of course, had left before the last four

Peterson children were born, so his surprise was comical, drawing a giggle from JulieAnn. With all of this talk about her family, JulieAnn couldn't help but wonder about Tandon's relationship with his father. It occurred to her that Tandon's return could be the opportunity for them to repair their relationship.

Aware she may be treading on thin ice she asked warily, "Have you seen your father?" and immediately, seeing his jaw clench, regretted her decision to bring it up. Not wanting to upset him further and risk ruining the day, she decided to change the conversation.

"I'm sorry. It's none of my business. Let's talk about something else," she offered, but felt his tension in the silence that followed.

As she searched for something to say Tandon broke through her thoughts, "I saw him this morning."

Surprised, JulieAnn turned to face him and tried to read his expression as he drove on, his gaze steady as he followed the winding road that led them down the side of the mountain, but he remained as poker faced as had his tone.

Wanting to encourage him she pressed tentatively, "How did it go?" Tandon's knuckles whitened slightly as he tightened, then flexed, his grip on the steering wheel.

Shrugging his shoulders he said, "It was just like old times."

"I'm sorry," she said.

Tandon looked at her for a moment, "Don't worry about it. I'm not."

JulieAnn was truly sorry for their troubles, but found she was disinclined, suddenly, to think about the relationship between the Bowman men, wanting rather to focus on the relationship, if one could call it that, between Tandon and herself. Each minute, indeed each second that they shared together was both a precious jewel, bright and shining, and dull white, grainy sands slipping through the slender neck of an hourglass, time in a bottle, unable to be stopped.

Then a crazy thought came to her. What if she could suspend time if only for a moment. The very notion of it appealed to her in such a way that she reveled in the idea, wondering, if she could, would she? And if so, for how long? Until whispered endearments melted his heart? Or if by staring hard into his eyes, she might convey to his soul her longing, in past years, to see his face, to hear his voice, to feel his touch? Would she be willing then to upright the hour glass? Risk the chance of being denied her dreams? Lose all hope that he would leave his life behind and come to her? Would it be fair? Could she really expect him to leave everything for her? Would it make him happy in the end? Or her? She had to concede that it would probably not.

For her own sake, she had to remain focused. To do otherwise would only invite renewed pain and loss. And, she reasoned with a final caution to her psyche, it would be better for her if she expected nothing and received nothing than to expect and wait never to know when or if, and receive nothing in return.

With a deep breath, she dismissed her thoughts, committing herself to this fine day with the mere promise of enjoying Tandon's company, knowing she would cherish every moment.

* * *

Tandon and JulieAnn pulled into a clearing just off the tail end of a private drive where a small home stood nearby, nestled within the walls if its tightly wooded enclosure. Tandon was aware that, with the nationalizing of the river, the house and all of its immediate surroundings would likely become government property. He felt a slight pang of sorrow for the owners since he guessed that they had chosen this area specifically for the hidden treasure that lay within.

Tandon reached into the truck pulling out the picnic basket that had shared the seat between them. After the visit with his father, he had gone to a deli to gather provisions for his lunch with JulieAnn. As he had waited for the lady behind the counter to wrap his smoked meat he had looked around and found a selection of locally crafted picnic baskets hanging from hooks in the ceiling. Knowing it would add to the traditional feel of a picnic he took one down and paid for it, his food, and drinks before heading out to the woman that awaited him.

JulieAnn had also reached into the truck, then stood, slinging the long handles of her bag over her shoulder, which to him, looked to be weighed down by a sizeable rock. "Can I carry your bag for you?" he asked, wondering how she kept from tipping over.

JulieAnn laughed, "Thanks, but it's not as

heavy as it looks," she said, easily reading his thoughts.

Tandon led her to an opening in the forest where a roughly cut trail wound visibly a short distance before disappearing out of sight. The trail was narrow enough that they had to walk in single file with Tandon taking the lead, assuring JulieAnn that he would keep a look out for snakes. He noted, with humor, that she made no argument against this as her eyes darted about at his words.

The two mile hike to their destination was slow going as they made their way along, ducking under branches and traversing fallen boulders from atop the hillside and trees that lay with massive girth across their path.

Although much of their time was spent watching the ground for safe passage, they did manage to stop often to approve the scenery. Their view in every direction en route being adorned with vibrant color from the blooming red woods and dogwood trees to the azaleas and irises growing in wild abandon along with others boasting yellows and whites and many rare arrangements that displayed themselves proudly, that both were at a loss to give a name to. Even the common trees and vegetation were dressing themselves in their finest green plumage - their leaves bright and fresh faced, unmarred by the weather and insects that would, too soon, wreak a natural but destructive havoc upon them.

Tandon kept up a light conversation as they moved along explaining to JulieAnn where they were headed and offering her bits of trivia about its history.

"Lost Valley is a famous place you know," he said to her over his shoulder.

"I remember hearing about it, but I'm ashamed to say I've never been here," she said.

"There's no better time than now. Judging from this creek here," Tandon said, nodding at the swift waters they trailed beside, in opposition to its current, "the spring rains have been heavy. Eden Falls should be impressive."

At her look of interest Tandon grinned, "But you won't see it until we've reached the end of the trail."

Along with the diverse assortment of vegetation were the occasional, but much grander in scale, displays of nature. On the opposite side of the creek from where Tandon stopped lay three boulders, massive in size. He noted how they resembled lost pieces of a puzzle as he pointed up to where they had apparently lost their hold on the bluff above.

JulieAnn took it all in with intrigue and especially so when they came upon what Tandon said was a natural bridge. There were two things to be noticed upon first sight of it - the swift stream flowing from it and a quite large and very dark opening. Both of which they saw from the large pool below.

Tandon saw JulieAnn's interested, but highly skeptical look, as though she had been had, somehow having missed the joke. The trail appeared to end here and it was apparent she thought that this was Eden Falls.

"Is this it?" she asked trying, but not quite succeeding, to hide the disappointment from her voice.

Tandon laughed, "Eden Falls? No."

"Then how, where…?"

"The trail continues on the other side," he said. "We have to climb up there," pointing to the darkness within, "and go through it."

Again JulieAnn looked disbelieving, "Are you sure?"

"Yep," he said enjoying her expression. He didn't tell her that you could actually make your way around, though with much effort, by continuing on through heavy foliage. He wanted her to experience it the right way.

JulieAnn looked up toward the wide ledge that appeared as black as a moonless night and squared her shoulders. "Okay then. Let's get going."

Tandon turned away, hiding his grin, and let her follow his lead as he looked for and found what appeared to be the easiest way to climb up. Once inside, they found they could stand up straight. The shelter was surprisingly dry but for the spring that ran out of the wall to merge with the stream.

"I can imagine the Indians taking shelter in here," Tandon said.

"I'm sure they did," she agreed.

"We know they were here because of the things that were found. The most interesting things though, were found up ahead at Cob Cave."

JulieAnn smiled, understanding immediately why it carried such a title, "Corn cobs," she said in a matter-of-fact tone.

Tandon smiled, "Exactly. They also found gourds, woven items, basketry, native seeds, arrowheads, and things of that nature."

JulieAnn smiled at his enthusiasm while marveling at his knowledge, "Shall we go find this great wonder?"

"Let's go."

They headed toward the beacon of light that signaled their point of exit.

After making their way back onto the trail they continued on, as did Tandon's lesson, "Did you know that National Geographic had been here in 1945?"

CHAPTER SIX

They heard the fluid progression of its course before they saw it and knew they were almost there. Stepping atop a large boulder, Tandon looked up from carefully placing his feet, and observed the source of it all.

Turning around he gave JulieAnn a hand up, "We're here," he said and formerly introduced her, "JulieAnn...Eden Falls," and heard her draw in a sharp breath as she lifted her eyes to the splendor before her.

Tandon could not help watching her as she took it all in for the first time. Her lips were parted in a smile of wonderment, her eyes, sparkling saucers as they held the waters reflection, her gaze following its descent as the white veil of liquid cascaded down the hillside's mossy, current beaten path, slamming onto its craggy surfaces to spill out over jutting ledges before finally settling into the earthen pool below.

The air was cooler here near the water and the breeze made by its surging rhythm blew JulieAnn's hair softly back from her face. She turned to him then, a radiant smile painting her face, "This is beautiful. I'm so glad we came here," she said.

Tandon's heart skipped a strange beat. "Me too," he said, returning her smile.

Ignoring the unexpected sensation, Tandon shifted the weight of the basket more comfortably to his grip. "I don't know about you, but I've worked up an appetite," he said.

"Mmm," JulieAnn sounded her agreement, nodding.

"Why don't we find a way across here and sit over there where it's flat," he said pointing across the pool.

"Okay," she agreed good-naturedly.

Tandon again led the way stepping gingerly from one rock to another offering JulieAnn a steady hand as she tried to keep from slipping on the slick surfaces.

Once across, they chose an area sheltered below an overhang of rock to set up their picnic. Together they emptied the basket of its contents, making quick work of their lunch, as they reminisced about old friends and their funny antics with JulieAnn updating him on their current whereabouts and activities having kept up relations with many of their schoolmates.

While Tandon watched her speak a strange current that was equally exciting and startling passed through him. They were feelings for JulieAnn, he knew that much, yet there was something missing. He didn't quite have it all and the harder he tried to grasp it the further it eluded him.

He tried concentrating on what she was saying, but found he was only hearing the soft tones of her voice. After a moment of quiet, Tandon realized she had finished her thoughts and he was thankful she didn't appear to be waiting for a response to a question he hadn't heard. Tandon looked around for a moment needing a distraction from the chaos of his thoughts.

As it would happen, it was JulieAnn herself who helped in his pursuit. "It looks like something's been digging here," she said.

Curious, Tandon followed her gaze, his interest automatically diverted. "Someone's been arrowhead digging here," he said and stood, hunching over so as not to hit his head on the narrowing ceiling and began scanning the ground for his own find.

Arrowhead digging was a hobby for him and he had acquired quite a collection over the years through his job. The only thing was that you could only keep what was found on private property. To do so on government property was against the law and would carry steep punishment.

"Don't you need tools to dig?" JulieAnn asked.

"Yes. Your basic screen and shovel will do, but sometimes if you're lucky you can spot one just lying on the surface. I've gotten quite a few that way," he said, remembering the friendly flack he got from fellow diggers envious of his luck as they dug, sweaty and dirty, often without good results of their own.

"This would have been a good place for the Indians to make them," he explained. "There's a lot of flint in the area."

JulieAnn walked over and joined him, copying his example as he bent down to brush the dirt around with his hands. "I'm not sure I know what I'm looking for," she said.

"There's a lot of different styles. Try looking for ones with pointed tips and notched ends. Some are smooth on the sides, others are jagged."

"Okay," she said kneeling in the dirt and putting all of her concentration into her search.

They scooted around the floor for a time before Tandon let out a hoot, "Bingo," he exclaimed coming over to show JulieAnn his discovery.

"This is a three inch Dalton point," he said excitedly, "and these serrations are nearly perfect in symmetry," he added running his finger lightly over the edges.

"You have a good eye," she said with admiration.

"It's just luck," he said humbly. "Here, it's for you," and stretched out his hand to her.

"Oh no, I couldn't. You found it. It's yours," she said, twisting her body away from his.

"Really, I have plenty. I want you to have it…a memento," he insisted taking a step toward her.

For a moment she looked at him, then at the arrowhead, before finally consenting to his offer. "Okay then. Thank you," she said, letting him place it in her hand.

He watched her admire it for a moment, then she said, "I should go pack up the basket."

Tandon was helping her replace its contents when her bag caught his attention. "Can I ask what you are hauling around in that bag?" he asked.

"Oh," she smiled, "it's my camera. It's kind of a hobby when I'm not using it for work. I drag it everywhere I go," she said. "And I'm glad I did today. This is a magnificent view to capture," she said and pulled out her 35mm Nikon camera with all of its attachable lenses.

Hanging its connecting strap around her neck she began snapping shots of the landscape from where she sat. "What I'd really like to do is go back across the pool and photograph the cave and waterfalls," she said.

"Done," Tandon said. "We'll just take all of this back with us."

Once again at the trail's side, JulieAnn left him to take her pictures. Tandon watched with amusement the lengths she would take to get "just the right shot," climbing rocks, forging up the hillside for a "view from above," and even hanging out over the pool with only one hand clasping a supposedly sturdy branch for support. A maneuver that had Tandon's heart pounding in fear.

When she was through she came back to where he sat with a satisfied look on her face and a sigh of pure pleasure. "If those turn out, which they should, they'll rank up there among my best to date," she said clearly pleased with her efforts.

"No doubt," he said with a chuckle, "though I've not seen your portfolio to judge," he teased. "Maybe you could make me copies of what you just took."

"Sure," she said, "I'll develop them myself."

Tandon was stunned, "You develop film too?"

"Oh, did I forget to mention that?" Seeing his raised brows she giggled, answering her own question. "I guess so. I took a course in it too." she explained.

"You're just full of surprises aren't you?" Tandon said.

JulieAnn laughed at that. "You just never can tell," she teased.

And at that moment his pulse leaped. A rush of emotion tore its way through Tandon making him catch his breath in a strangling moment. He felt suddenly dizzy.

He was in love with JulieAnn!

"It's getting late and we have a way to go. We should get going…don't you think?" she asked.

Tandon blinked hard, clearing his throat, "I'm sorry?" he said in a raspy voice.

"It's getting late. Maybe we should go?" she repeated lifting the camera strap off over her head.

Tandon glanced at his watch, not really seeing its face, but somehow noticing the dirt thick on his hands from digging, "You're right. I'll just go rinse this dirt off first," he said.

Tandon walked over to the waterfall, leaning in to allow the clear, crisp water to wash over his hands. Before turning back, he gazed upwards along the falls, allowing the fine mist to cool his face, and giving himself a moment to process these new feelings. As he did so he heard a click from behind him.

Turning then, he saw JulieAnn standing where

he had left her with one foot on the ground, the other on a rock beside her for balance. She was lowering the camera slowly from her sights while continuing to look at him, unsmiling.

"Does that thing have a timer?" he asked just loud enough for her to hear him.

"Yes," she said nodding.

"If you like, we could take a picture together. Another memento."

JulieAnn hesitated for only a moment before agreeing. "Sure," she said.

Tandon waited while JulieAnn set the camera on a rock and focused its sights to where he stood. After setting the timer she scurried over to stand beside him. Impulsively, Tandon reached an arm around her waist, happy to find no resistance.

"Smile," she advised through her own, already positioned, features.

Tandon obeyed, but could not, with his new discovery, keep his gaze from straying to her.

As if sensing his attention, JulieAnn turned her gaze to his, her chin slightly raised, a few dark wisps of hair blowing gently across her cheek, and a contented glow in her eyes.

Click. Flash.

They started slightly at the sound, laughing softly, their eyes never leaving the others, and with Tandon's arm never loosening its hold.

"Kiss her," his heart screamed, but his mind fought him, "Don't start something you can't finish. Don't lead her on…you are leaving soon. It won't be fair to either of you." Did she just move closer? She is so beautiful. I love her. I love JulieAnn.

The Chimney Still Stands

Tandon felt the warmth of her hands on his arms and without further thought, bent his head. He felt her lips, warm and soft, as he pressed his mouth to hers. Everything he had ever suppressed, that being the truth, every vain attempt to tell himself something different, was all for naught. JulieAnn was what he wanted, what he needed. And now, standing before him, wrapped snug in his embrace, was his future.

* * *

It was JulieAnn who broke the kiss, pulling back slightly, still within his hold. She opened her eyes slowly as tears, pooled behind her lids, poured unchecked down her cheeks. Looking at Tandon, she was overcome by the emotion she saw revealed there, the intensity of his gaze making it impossible to concentrate on anything else. Sights and sounds her senses had been tuned to earlier were now hushed. The hypnotic rhythm of the waterfall, songs of a feathered choir, the soft rustling of leaves, all these were lost in a dream. Her hour glass had truly been tipped and time stood at a standstill.

She waited, breathless, for the words to follow. The words she was sure he was trying, silently, to convey to her. She felt it deep in her soul as surely as if he had spoken them. But the dream wasn't complete. Not until he confirmed it, could she be certain.

Silently she gave her request to God, over and over she repeated it. Then, as though in answer to her prayer, Tandon immediately opened his mouth and spoke her name, "JulieAnn," he said in a throaty whisper.

"Yes?" she asked, hopeful. She gazed passionately up at him, her heart pounding an incredible rhythm. The loneliness of the past sixteen years was entirely forgotten as she waited to hear those three glorious words.

Tandon's mouth moved to speak, but no sound came. JulieAnn watched him try again and yet again; saw the emotion in his face changing as his passion turned to pain. Then his arms about her waist loosened until they stood, separated, one before the other.

Tandon turned away, leaving JulieAnn standing alone and confused. There was no mistaking what he had been about to say to her. She was sure of that. What went wrong?

Her surroundings reclaimed their attention with the suddenness of cold water being doused over her head. The cool breeze sent a shiver down her spine and she unconsciously hugged her arms about her protectively.

"We better get going," Tandon said and walked back to pick up the basket leaving JulieAnn to follow.

Their ride back to town was a silent one, each lost in their own thoughts.

For JulieAnn, the bittersweet hours they had shared were played over and over in her mind. Had she misread his intentions? Had her own hopes led her to see something that was not really there? She felt more alone now than she had before his return...no longer confident of herself, but instead questioned her own intuitions, her own part in this apparent fantasy she had come to believe in.

The silence was awkward and JulieAnn was relieved when, finally, the town came into view. They were soon parked in front of her office and instead of waiting for Tandon to come around and open her door, as he had been doing, JulieAnn herself opened the door and quickly stepped out.

Tandon met her on the sidewalk and walked beside her to the door. Wordlessly, JulieAnn unlocked it and stepped inside setting her bag on her desk as Tandon followed her in, leaving the door open behind him.

"Thank you for the picnic. I had a terrific time," she said in truth.

Tandon smiled stuffing his hands into his pockets. "Me too," he said and continued to look at her for a time before turning away.

She wasn't sure what he was thinking. He seemed to not know what to say or do next.

Finally he turned to her with a deep breath and said, "I have to be out of town for a few days. I need to check on my team and catch up on some work. I'll be back sometime Friday."

JulieAnn nodded her head somewhat surprised. She hadn't considered he would be gone for so long. "Okay," she said softly.

"Can I call you when I get back?" he asked.

His question perked her up a bit. "I'd like that," she said smiling.

"Okay," he said then sighed, "I guess I'll...talk to you Friday then."

"Friday," she confirmed.

Tandon stepped closer to her, hesitating before bending his head to hers. JulieAnn tipped her head back and looked into his warm hazel eyes, her heart melting all over again, before he kissed her. It was a gentle kiss, simple and non-inviting, but JulieAnn's arms starting to rise of their own volition. Tandon pulled back, seeming not to notice her intent, and took a safe step away.

Without a word, they said their goodbyes. Then JulieAnn watched from the doorway as he pulled his truck away.

CHAPTER SEVEN

Over the next few days Tandon devoted himself to his work, the constant reliance upon each day's routine becoming a thankful distraction, bringing with it the comfort of familiarity and security; a positive and a surety when all other nuances of life were in an upheaval. His ability to remain busy and focused on such a tight schedule was not only doable, but a blessing in disguise that he sought with fervor.

From Wednesday afternoon until noon Friday Tandon met with the members of his team, himself an active participant in the retrieval process of his mission. Unlike the men under his charge, whose particular roles kept them somewhat stationary, Tandon's duties covered the whole of four counties spanning the length of the river, with traveling to and fro taking up much of his time. Not only was there distance to contend with but meetings to be arranged and carried out whereby the gathering and reporting of information was conducted.

Although they made up the majority of the team, surveyors were not the only professionals to have joined in their efforts. There was another class of the Park Service whose responsibility it was given to report on the quality of ground water and minerals, forest resources, roads and highways, population and education, and also very importantly, that of land use - the necessity of it being to judge whether or not the land would be capable of bringing a return investment that would prove to be sufficient enough to advocate its continual use. Without that evidence to indicate progress for the country, Congress would not pass the bill.

Tandon knew that, besides the personal loss to the landowners, the smaller outlying towns were near ghost town status and the opportunities afforded to them by the nationalizing of the river would be tremendous. He himself had been witness to these effects. The small, unknown, blink and you miss it towns - these have awakened, flourishing under the yearly growth of tourism and the steady rise in population as people's desire of these fresh faced areas draws them in.

Basing intuition on history Tandon could envision, even now, the future surrounding the would-be Buffalo National River. There would be canoe rentals for the spring floaters, bed and breakfasts, RV parks, and log cabin rentals. Shops selling original works from the local talent would spring forth. Artists from every walk of life would come here seeking inspiration and opportunities for employment would rise.

Tandon felt certain that, when all was said and done and folks settled down to the idea, the general feeling would be one of appreciation. And though he was an admirer and advocate of history, he was also in favor of progress. This was an area that he saw as being in desperate need of that with really no other way around it save the one that was currently in the making.

Another area in desperate need of progress was in Tandon's own personal life. Each evening, after the day's duties had been fulfilled and Tandon retired to his rented room, there being a new one each day, the events of the past week would resurface to be picked and prodded until, unsettled, he would fall into distracted sleep.

Prior to his arrival in Arkansas, Tandon had had plenty of time to think not only of the job at hand but also about his father and JulieAnn. He knew he would see them, had even imagined the conversations that would take place, but in each case he had felt confident and in control, his feelings unchanged. His self-preserving intentions, however, had quickly flown out the window when his theoretical views were met with reality. The most unexpected of these came with a certain blow to his senses, an awakening of sorts that was both troubling and comforting.

Thinking about his father had always been a difficult thing for Tandon. It was, in fact, an issue he has had to force upon himself, but unlike in the past, when his solicited thoughts had come from that of an independent and defiant teenager's perspective, he now found himself, in more recent days, challenged by marked influences that were redefining his opinion. It was his visit, or rather, his confrontation with his father Tuesday that, in spite of having to raise his own defenses, had made quite an impact on him.

Over these past few nights Tandon took the opportunity to mull over his father's words, trying to pinpoint the underlying message until, after much trial and error, he thought he understood. Underneath his father's shield of anger were open wounds of bitterness and defeat. The passing of time and age, while pierced with loneliness, all made for a losing battle. His father, in Tandon's surmise, had become an enemy of himself.

And suddenly Tandon saw his father through his mother's eyes. He remembered her words to him, to love his father for who he is and who he is human. A frail, tired man whose purpose and worth have been torn away by loss in one form or another.

Tandon understood his father's shame for him, his son. The loss of his wife, and soon his home, are both intertwined with him. Though he wasn't the cause of either upset, he had played a hand in their terminal end. Humbled by these revelations, Tandon was determined to somehow make amends with his father, and he had until Sunday afternoon to figure out how to go about it.

During these same nights his thoughts had also revolved around JulieAnn. He had planned only for a quick visit with her, similar to the one at his mother's funeral, but it seemed nothing he expected would be realized.

From the moment he saw her name in the paper, then having seen her in person at the NPS meeting, he knew nothing would go as planned. He wasn't sure why this visit was so different, but he found he was incapable, and disinclined, to change it.

He had surprised himself by asking her out, though at the time it seemed a natural thing to do. And as always, when he thought about it, his mind went straight to their kiss. The atmosphere that afternoon had changed when he had mentally acknowledged his love for her. Hours had been spent since then questioning it. It seemed almost ridiculous that, after so many years, only a few hours in her company would bring him to such a conclusion. But he knew it was for real. Why then, couldn't he tell her? He had wanted to after their kiss, but the words wouldn't come. Maybe he subconsciously thought she would think oddly of him, not believing in his sincerity. That she too would question the timing and think it less than it was.

He couldn't let it go and decided he needed to tell her. Time was running out though, and that was not the only dilemma. They lived different lives and in different places. Should he ask her to go back with him? Could they have a long distance relationship? These were questions he didn't know the answers to. In the meantime, he decided, he would sleep on it and hope something would come to him.

* * *

JulieAnn had made it to her brother's baseball

game Tuesday night, cheering with fellow friends and family members of the players as Jess put their team on top with a three run homer in the first inning. Her decision to go at the last minute had more to do with herself, personally, than with her brother. It turned out to be the right decision, the right distraction, for a while.

She spent the time wisely, visiting with the folks around her on the bleachers and those she met in passing as she made her way to and from the concession stand. At one point, as she half listened to a couple of ladies who had stopped her to gossip, JulieAnn realized she was looking around for Tandon. She had mentioned to him that he could come to her brother's game, but he had never said whether or not he would. She never did see him that night and found herself disheartened by the fact.

After the game she had visited with her brother for a minute, declining his invitation to the barbecue. "Thanks, but I'll go home. I'm pretty tired," she said, which was true, but mostly she had wanted to dodge the questions Jess was sure to ask.

Surprisingly that night she slept hard and without distraction, the fresh air and exercise being a bit more than she was used to. The following days were back to work as usual for JulieAnn as she and Rebecca readied the weekly paper with its general tidbits of information. With it set to print they worked on the headline for the cover story.

JulieAnn was at a loss for some time as she decided whether to include Tandon's history with the town or not. If she had not known him personally, she knew she would have, but the fact that she did know him fueled a particular dilemma. She knew that word of him had probably gotten around to most people by now and that if the fact was not mentioned in the paper, it might appear as being inconsequential, which to the concerned population it was not, and Letters to the Editor would start pouring in. She did think that to include the information would only be leading the facts astray. Tandon, alone, was not the issue no matter how strongly the people might lean toward it. The fact remained, a stranger could have come and performed the same duties Tandon had, it would change nothing.

Finally, based on those rational estimations, she made her final decision on the latter. By Friday afternoon the story had been written and the papers printed. All were set for release Monday morning.

As they were getting ready to leave JulieAnn became aware, again, that Rebecca seemed to have something on her mind. She had seen her looking thoughtfully at her throughout the day, but dismissed it as her work claimed much of her time. Now, with nothing more to occupy her, she gave Rebecca her full attention. "Becca, did you want to ask me something?"

Rebecca looked guiltily at JulieAnn, her face flushing, "Um, no. It's really none of my business," she said and turned away trying to escape JulieAnn's inquiring look.

JulieAnn cocked her head wondering what could have brought about this strange reaction. "Becca, you can talk to me. What is it?" she encouraged.

Rebecca looked shyly at her, "I was just wondering," she said and quickly looked away, flicking her wrist in a dismissive way. "It's none of my business anyway," she repeated.

Now, JulieAnn's curiosity was definitely piqued, "You know you're my best friend. You can ask me anything." When there was no response she added, "Really. Don't worry."

Visibly struggling to summon up enough courage Rebecca finally squared her shoulders and faced JulieAnn, "I know you love him," she said and when she saw JulieAnn's brows raise, added hastily, "I mean, the man you went out with the other day. I saw it in your eyes."

JulieAnn was taken aback at that. It was not at all what she had expected, although an actual idea had never formed concerning the contents of Rebecca's thoughts.

Rebecca went on in a rush, "I only say that because I've heard talk. Nasty, nasty rumors. And I'm sure none of them are true," she hastened to add holding out her hands in a pleading gesture, "but they've made me wonder, worry," she corrected quickly, "about you."

JulieAnn laughed, "There's nothing to worry about," she said leaning in toward Rebecca, "or wonder about."

"So you do love him? I was right?"

JulieAnn let that sink in for a moment before saying, "Yes, I do. You are right." But instead of looking happy for her, Rebecca looked even more concerned. "Why am I getting the feeling that this is a problem?" JulieAnn asked.

"Well, it's just that," Rebecca looked frustrated at her own inability to find the right words, "I don't want you to get hurt."

"Are we talking about the gossip, or Tandon?"

"Both!" Rebecca said, her answer bursting from her as though she correctly answered the winning question on a TV game show. "I mean," Rebecca looked contrite for a moment, "oh, I don't know what I mean." Then after a pause, "Yes, I do!"

Rebecca's voice became a whisper as she relieved herself of her burdensome thoughts, while at the same time not wishing to hurt her friend, "JulieAnn, he's taking people's land." When JulieAnn opened her mouth to correct that statement Rebecca quickly jumped in to rephrase herself. "Well he's working for them. And some of those are my friends, and yours. Doesn't that bother you?"

JulieAnn answered quickly, "Of course it bothers me. But Becca, we don't know for a fact that the bill will be passed. As for Tandon, we can't blame him. His job is to survey, not make the final decision. Should we be blamed for printing a story if one half of it looks truthfully, but unfavorably, on a particular person or issue? Of course not. You and I, and Tandon, all share the same job - to report our findings. Nothing more. We are no more responsible for the outcome of certain situations than he is."

Rebecca looked as if she were trying to make up her mind as to which to believe. The rumors she had been hearing were so heated and passionate she had found her spine stiffening in defense of them. But JulieAnn, too, had a point and that was causing a huge conflict of interest.

Rebecca rubbed the back of her neck as a dull ache began spreading. "I understand what you're saying," she said, "but people will believe what they want to believe and that could cause a lot of problems for your relationship with Tandon. I just don't want to see you suffer those consequences."

JulieAnn walked over to Rebecca and gave her a hug. "I appreciate your concern, I really do, but you shouldn't worry." JulieAnn stepped back a bit, "Truthfully, I'm not sure where I stand with Tandon, but if we do move forward, as a couple, I'm sure that after a while talk will die down."

"I hope so," Rebecca said, "I do wish the best for you."

JulieAnn could see the sincerity in her friend and smiled her appreciation, "Thanks, Becca," she said giving her another hug. "Well, I guess we can call it a day."

"Sounds good to me," Rebecca agreed.

After saying their goodbyes and wishing each other a good weekend they headed out to their vehicles and parted ways, both women growing serious in thought as they each had much to think about.

CHAPTER EIGHT

It was late afternoon, Friday, as Tandon wound his way off the mountains nearing the outskirts of Jasper. He could have made better time and been in his hotel room in Harrison by now, but he had taken a leisurely pace, enjoying the scenery while trying to relax. The next couple of days would be stressful in and of themselves, but could be made even more so if things didn't go in his favor.

A few yards up ahead, which he was able to read as he drew nearer to it, was a homemade billboard made by a local restaurant boasting the goodness of its down home southern cooking. Normally that would have appealed to him. Just the thought of a heaping plate full of chicken fried steak drenched in white country gravy with green beans and buttered rolls made his mouth water.

Despite his growing appetite, however, he was tired and the thought of eating another meal out, alone, just didn't hold any appeal for him tonight. Besides, his hotel room was equipped with a small kitchen area that was suitable for putting together his own meal, after which he planned to call JulieAnn.

Arriving in town Tandon pulled into the parking lot of Jimmy's General Store. It was the kind that didn't carry a large selection of sort but the basic essentials to last you until your next big trip to Harrison. Tandon remembered it fondly. As a young boy he had come here with his parents buying anything from toilet paper and ice cream to chainsaw oil and fire crackers. What he had really looked forward to then was seeing Jimmy, the burly old timer who was clever with the jokes and told them while gnawing on a piece of rock candy. Tandon was always encouraged to help himself to the same, while Jimmy never accepted the nickel it cost.

As Tandon stepped out of the NPS truck and headed toward the store, a group of older men, sitting together on aged wooden benches before the store's windows, stopped their conversation, observing him closely. Without staring back as blatantly as they, he did observe one man as he spoke some words to his neighbor that Tandon couldn't quite catch, while pulling a wad of tobacco from the tin he held, stuffing his lip thick with the stuff.

Tandon reached for the door and with a nod to the men opened the wooden screen door allowing it to spring shut behind him. Despite the cooling temperature outside, the air in the store remained thick and stuffy, circulated only by the industrial fan at the end of the long room. Tandon looked about without seeing anyone. Thinking one of the men outside would be in shortly to ring up his purchases, he went about studying the shelves for his dinner.

After loading an arm with some goods he walked around the aisle and looked up to see Jimmy stepping out from the back office. Tandon's face lit up at the sight of the old man who had aged little from what he could remember.

"Mr. Nichols, how are you?" Tandon walked up to Jimmy and offered his hand, but his greeting was ignored. Tandon thought that, perhaps, the man's hearing had diminished through the years, so he repeated himself, louder this time.

"I heard you the first time," Jimmy said.

Tandon grimaced, "I'm sorry. It's been a long time. Maybe you don't remember me? I'm…"

"I know who you are," Jimmy interrupted, giving Tandon, in his NPS uniform, a scathing once over.

Taken aback at Jimmy's abrupt manner, Tandon said nothing as the older man turned away, book and pen in hand, and stepped into an aisle to take inventory.

At first Tandon wasn't sure what had just happened until he was struck by a thought, and suddenly it became apparent that talk had circulated about him in the days since the meeting and that folks were taking it to heart. Having always been somewhat of a spokesman for the locals, Jimmy's reaction made it a tell-all in the community. He knew then that attitudes would be similar throughout the area. Tandon felt a sense of unbalance creeping over him. As the seconds ticked by and visions of scornful looks and slamming doors plagued his mind, he grew tense, feeling out of place.

More than a little disheartened, Tandon went to the head of the aisle Jimmy was in. Not knowing what he was going to say, he began simply, "Mr. Nichols," and when he didn't get a response he pressed on, "Mr. Nichols...I'm sorry."

"Like hell you are," Jimmy said and moved to the next aisle.

Tandon did the same, "Mr. Nichols...Jimmy, I"

"Jimmy's for friends. Mr.'s for strangers...like you," Jimmy said without ever looking up from his book.

Another awkward moment passed as Tandon stood there, dumbfounded. His brain seemed to have stopped functioning. He couldn't think of anything meaningful to say. He knew no amount of arguing would make a difference and it appeared casual conversation was out of the question, but it seemed something needed to be said.

Before he could think of what that was, Jimmy walked past him and back to the counter with Tandon trailing hesitantly behind. As he reached the counter, Jimmy turned to the wall behind him, took down a sign and placed it flat on the counter before Tandon. It read, "This establishment reserves the right to refuse service to anyone for any reason."

Tandon looked at the goods shelved on his arm. He had forgotten all about them until now. He looked back at Jimmy, who stared straight at him, "Your money's no good here," he said and dipped his head pointedly to the load Tandon held.

Stunned and embarrassed Tandon placed his collection on the counter, then looked up at Jimmy who had clearly dismissed him as he picked up the goods and moved to replace them on the shelves.

Tandon went to the door, now eager to leave, and stepped out into the blessed rush of cool air. After a brief pause to get his bearings, he stepped forward. At the same moment he heard a spitting sound just as brown juice flew in front of his lowering boot. He turned to the men on the benches, spotting the culprit with the grimy juice dribbling onto his beard and glared hard at him until, frustrated and sensing a lost cause, he turned away and headed for his truck, now only too happy to get out of town.

* * *

When JulieAnn arrived home Friday evening it was to find Jess' truck parked in her drive with him sitting on her front porch, his feet crossed and resting on the railing.

By the time she had opened the trunk to retrieve her groceries Jess had reached her side, "If you're going to cook me dinner, the least I can do is carry it in," he said.

"Ha, ha," she returned. "This is for Gram's birthday dinner tomorrow. You didn't forget about it, did you?" she asked sounding very maternal.

"Oh, is that tomorrow?" he teased, getting a piercing look in return as they stepped into the house.

"You better..."

"Yeah, I remember," Jess said, handing his

sister the groceries as she placed them in the refrigerator and cupboards.

When they had finished Jess popped the cap off a Seven Up and took a seat at the kitchen table while JulieAnn warmed up some soup. Without beating around the bush Jess asked, "So, how did it go with Tandon?"

JulieAnn had expected the question when she saw his truck. She hadn't spoken to him since the game and knowing that he'd wanted to ask then she was surprised it had taken him three days to get around to it. "It went well," she said. "We went to Lost Valley. Did you know there's a natural bridge? There's even a waterfall and cave. The Indians used to live in. It's quite large. I took some pictures. I haven't developed them yet, but you'll be the first to see them when they're finished." Jess was looking at her funny, making her a bit self-conscious. "Why are you looking at me like that?" she asked.

JulieAnn's uncharacteristically vague answer had Jess suspicious right off the bat. "Did he try anything?"

"Jess!" she scolded.

Jess threw his hands up, "Hey, I trust you. I just don't trust him."

Suddenly, Jess was on his feet hovering before her in what she immediately recognized as, "his actors pose". Groaning in mock distress, as though what was to come would be somehow painful to witness, she braced herself, unable to keep from grinning in anticipation of his theatrics.

"I know how guys think, see. The plan is to

whisk you away to some secluded place, far from civilization, to…let's say, oh…a cave for instance, with the soothing and romantic sounds of a waterfall all around you," Jess flicked on the kitchen faucet for effect. "He then wines and dines you, feeding you chocolates," grabbing a handful of M&M's from the bowl on the counter he drops one in her mouth and shoves the rest into his own and continues, "and raw oysters,"

JulieAnn scrunched her face at that. "Then he tries to loosen you up with a little bubbly." He took hold of his Seven Up, holding it under his nose, "It tickles your nose. You giggle drunkenly," with female flourish he twitches his nose and giggles.

"Stop," JulieAnn managed to choke out, "it was nothing like that." Jess gave her a look that said simply, "Maybe not exactly, but probably close enough."

"Did he kiss you?" he asked.

JulieAnn sobered abruptly and swung around to stir the soup, needing time to compose herself.

"Oh Jul's," he said, correctly interpreting her response.

Thankfully the phone rang at that moment. Quickly she grabbed the receiver off the wall. "Hello," she said a little too loudly.

"Hi."

Her brother was all but forgotten as she recognized the voice on the other end of the line. "Hi," she returned softly.

"I hope I'm not interrupting anything," Tandon said.

"No, not at all. I was just warming up some

soup. Have you been back long?" JulieAnn asked.

Just then her brother motioned to her, mouthing, "Is that Tandon? Let me talk to him." She gave him a quick scowl and turned her back to him.

Distracted, she had missed Tandon's answer, and hoping he hadn't commented similarly she asked, "Would you like to come over for dinner?"

"Thanks, but no. I'm pretty tired and probably wouldn't be great company right now."

"I understand."

"I was hoping I could see you tomorrow...if you were interested."

JulieAnn was definitely interested. "I'd like that," she said and turned, then spotting the greens on the counter she was planning to make for the party and an idea came to her. "How would you like to go with me to a party tomorrow?"

Jess jumped up from the chair he'd been sitting in and waved frantically at her, mouthing, "No. Don't you dare! JulieAnn..." and looking very nearly ready to explode.

Watching him, JulieAnn wondered what she was doing but couldn't make herself stop. "It's a birthday party for my grandmother, Annabelle. She'll be seventy-five so we're all getting together at their place."

"Oh. I don't know about that," Tandon said.

"It'll be alright. They'd love to see you again, and you can meet the youngest members." Jess was still motioning to her, now adding the slit throat movement and throwing his arms in the air when she continued to ignore him.

When Tandon didn't answer she pleaded, "Please? I know what you're thinking, but you don't have to worry. Everyone'll be on their best behavior. I promise," she said, shooting a meaningful glance in her brother's direction.

She heard a chuckle at that. "What do you say? You can pick me up around one."

"I say, okay. Why not. It'll be good to see everyone again."

"Oh good. I'm so glad," she said, beaming.

"One o'clock it is then."

"Great. See you then," she said, and hung up, elated, until she turned and faced her brother.

* * *

Tandon hung his head and groaned. What was he getting himself into? He had spent the last hour, since arriving at his hotel room, trying to decide how, and when, to confess his love to JulieAnn and had decided to call and see if she would be willing to see him the next day. The idea was to be alone with her somewhere so he could admit his feelings, and hopefully, if his instincts were right, she would admit the same and they could go from there, working together on the tough decisions. But after getting up the nerve to call, and having it fall apart before his eyes, he wished he could just, well, escape.

He was not at all thrilled with the idea of going to her grandmother's birthday party and it was not only because he had wanted some privacy with JulieAnn, but he knew, all too well, that her grandparents would be one of the landowners to lose their home. And being, himself, the center of reproach was not what he called fun. But JulieAnn was convincing and his need to see her was overpowering. He just hoped they could find some time alone together before the night ended.

Tandon's stomach grumbled then so loudly that he was glad no one else was around to hear it. He had lost his appetite after seeing Jimmy and had not, as of yet, gotten any dinner. Tandon grabbed his wallet and room key and went down to the hotel restaurant. Only a few people were seated. It looked like the place was preparing to close so he ordered a burger and side dish to go and headed back to his room.

As he turned the key in the lock, the phone rang. He considered ignoring it, but instead walked to the bedside and answered it, "Hello?"

"Tandon, it's Greg Zimmerman. How's everything going?"

Tandon sat heavily on the bed. He was not in the mood to talk business but answered, "Fine. The pace is going along steadily."

"Good, good. Did you talk with the landowners yet?"

"I did, Monday," Tandon said.

"So how'd it go? Did you make any headway with them?" Greg asked.

Tandon wished wholeheartedly that he could have said yes. It would have made things a lot easier. "It's hard to say," was all he said.

"Do you think being a native has worked in our favor?" Greg wanted to know.

Tandon was hesitant to answer because he knew what it would mean to the Park Service, although it would make little difference to them in their fight to own it.

He answered honestly, "No sir, I don't believe it has. In fact, I think it may have made it worse."

There was a moment of silence before Greg said, "Well Tandon, I won't say I'm not disappointed. We had high hopes when we sent you down there. Not that it's your fault, mind you," Greg added quickly. Too quickly for Tandon. "I'm sure you can see where we're coming from."

Tandon was instantly on guard. Surely his failure to win over the hearts of the community would not be cause for demotion…or worse. "Sir, I did my best." Tandon hurriedly played the meeting back in his mind, recalling the questions and answers, certain he had properly informed them of what was to come. True, he hadn't gone out of his way to be overly friendly with anyone, but sucking up wasn't his style. He was merely the informant.

"I'm sure you did Tandon," Greg said.

"I hope you're not suggesting…" Tandon said, leaving the rest unsaid primarily because he couldn't say the words.

"Hold on there now. I'm not suggesting anything. Your position is safe," Greg said.

Tandon closed his eyes and let out a quiet breath of relief.

"We had just thought that once these bills had been passed, which you can bet your hat will happen, that you might like to be permanently relocated to the Ozarks as superintendent of the Buffalo National River."

Tandon's head snapped up. Of course until

now, which Greg was unaware of, he had tried to stay as far away as possible, but now, with the hopes that JulieAnn returned his affection, he would have the chance to start a life with her…here. He couldn't believe it. Suddenly life looked a lot brighter.

"Are you serious?" Tandon asked.

Greg laughed, "I sure am. I can see you're interested."

"Yes sir, I am. I should tell you though, there's a lot riding on that decision."

"Well, get your priorities together and give me the heads up when you figure it out."

"I will sir. And thank you," Tandon said, and meant it.

"Sure. You've earned it."

"Thank you, sir."

"Come and see me first thing when you get back."

"I will sir," Tandon said and hung up.

For a long time after that Tandon sat there contemplating all the possibilities, going over all the what-if's. He covered all the positives and negatives, picturing all the scenarios and in the end all he knew was that it was a game of chance. All he could do was hope for the best.

CHAPTER NINE

Tandon bolted upright in bed. Something had woken him. The room was black and still. The only sound - heavy breathing. The only visible thing - the glowing hands of the clock. A sudden blast echoed through the room. He jumped, startled. Whipping his head toward the sound, he heard a pop in his neck. The pain reverberated through his head. Another blast. Again, he jumped. Someone, or something, had hit the door.

Tandon slid cautiously off the bed. As he reached the door an insistent pounding erupted from the other side. Flinging off the chain, he wrenched open the door. A mass of bodies, their faces illuminated, swarmed around him, forcing him backwards into the room.

He saw her then - his mother. Panic gripped him. She shouldn't be here. None of them should. He recognized them all - his parents, JulieAnn, the man in the booth, Jimmy Nichols, Greg

Zimmerman, the cops, the older woman at the meeting, and all the rest. He stumbled back, his gaze sweeping from side to side, searching their unblinking eyes.

Then they spoke, their words - harsh and accusing, soft and loving. Their faces - looming, each in turn. "You left us…swindling government…follow your dreams…persuade them…let the river be…meet for lunch."

In unison they accused, "Traitor."

A sudden flash from JulieAnn's camera blinded him.

"Follow your heart…forget I wear a badge…proud of you…this is beautiful."

Another flash. The attack quickened.

"Traitor."

Spitoo. Tobacco spattered his face.

"Like hell…your money's no good here…my home."

Closer and closer they came. Backwards he struggled. Faster they spoke, each voice tripping over the other. Their faces - brilliant.

His heart raced as fear ripped through him, his mind screaming for escape.

"Relocate…love you son…bite your head off…traitor…haven't bothered." Spitoo.

His legs were hindered - his flight stopped. His knees buckled as an unseen edge tipped his balance. Falling backwards, helpless, he landed with a thud.

Another flash then total darkness, and for a moment, silence. He reached up. Six inches. Crack. Flesh clashed with wood, his knuckles grieving in pain. He searched blindly, his shoulders shifting a half inch to the left, half to the right. His feet pressed flat, the top of his head - pressure. He was stuck - snug. It was a coffin. He was buried alive.

Desperation consumed him. He wanted out. He pounded and pounded, dull thud after dull thud. No one heard. He screamed, "Help…somebody help me…" No one answered. He felt terminal pressure, heavy on his chest. A frigid blanket wrapped around him, seeping deep, far into his marrow. Then, abruptly, it ended. All was quiet and still. For a moment.

Suddenly he fell, dropping lower and lower into the abyss. The heat was excruciating - pain beyond torment. He thrashed wildly, "Nooo…"

From someplace far off into the distance, he heard a muffled scream. It grew louder, closer now and horrible until, with a start, Tandon woke, his eyes bulging wide and frightened as he jerked wildly, tangled in a twisted confusion of material. He jumped up from the floor scanning the room, his chest heaving, his skin clammy, posture defensive, until gradually realizing he was awake and that it was his own wailing that had woken him.

The room was still somewhat dark, but less of a threat as sunlight poured in through the crack of the heavy curtains. He jerked them open, then swung around, still on guard. Still feeling the effects of the dream. Slowly his mind cleared and his sanity returned as he sat on the bed, resting his forehead on his palms and let out a deep breath. Tandon had never been one for analyzing dreams, in fact he had never had one that called for it, but there was something about this nightmare that had him in goose bumps. He didn't believe in omens either. If he did, he was certain this would be one that called for a quick change of lifestyle. But fortunately, a dream was just that, a dream, and it needed no further rationalizing. So, shaking off the chill, Tandon decided the most logical thing would be to get on with reality and put this dream behind him as he would with any other.

Combing his fingers through his hair he stood, thinking about the day ahead, a crooked smile dancing across his face when a vision of JulieAnn came to mind. Then a nervous knot balled up in his stomach as he realized the time was near when he'd have to take the risk and tell her how he felt. He knew he could do it. The only problem was that he didn't know how she would react. He told himself, "The day will pass quickly and by the end of it you'll know. Then you can relax." It calmed him somewhat.

"Oh no," he said out loud, suddenly remembering Grandmother Annabelle and her party. He couldn't show up empty handed. He needed to get her a gift.

He turned to see what time it was and gasped. Ten-thirty! He shot around the room, tossing and grabbing and finally headed to the shower. He had two and a half hours until he picked up JulieAnn. But first, the gift. And he had no idea what that would be.

* * *

This morning JulieAnn woke early, eager to start the day. She had gotten herself ready so quickly that she had nothing left to do with the remainder of her time but fidget in anticipation. As the morning wore on though, she started feeling anxious and found herself repeatedly pushing the faces of Jess and Rebecca out of her mind, only to have them sneak up again and again, fragments of their conversations filtering through, forcing upon her the need to distract herself. She picked up a novel she had been reading and went out to the front porch, but found herself rereading the same page over and over. Sighing, she set it down thinking a walk around the block might help.

She had just started to relax when a man, rocking on his porch with his wife, called out to her. She decided to keep walking, hoping not to seem rude by dodging a visit, but slowed down and waved to the couple, "Good morning, Mr. and Mrs. Hatfield. It's a beautiful day."

"Hello, dear," the woman called, returning the gesture.

"Looking forward to that paper Monday," the man said. "It's a shame what's going on around here. The world's just not the place it used to be."

JulieAnn smiled respectfully, "We'll have it to you Monday morning," she said waving, not wanting to be pulled into the lengthy discussion that that comment was leading into, and had returned home soon after feeling no less distracted than when she had left.

JulieAnn lifted the edge of the lace curtain that was on the front door for, close to, the hundredth time the past half hour looking for Tandon's truck. There were still five minutes until he was due, but she was restless, suffering on pins and needles.

Quickly, she ran to the bathroom mirror and checked her appearance. Satisfied, as she was the three times before that, she headed back down the hallway.

There was a knock on the door and she started, her heart fluttering in response. She knew it was Tandon and her intuitions were confirmed when she saw the perfect outline of his profile through the delicate material. JulieAnn caught her breath at the sight of him. The rush of emotions she had felt at the meeting were there again and she felt as though she were drowning in their depths. This time, however, and unlike the meeting, there were more complicated emotions cresting over, blocking her view of the smaller, more harmless, currents that struggled from behind, determined to be seen.

Ashamed with herself for allowing others' unschooled judgments to cloud her mind, she pushed them all aside and swung the door wide as Tandon prepared to knock again.

"Hi," they said together as was their habit of late.

Tandon swung his arm around from behind him and handed JulieAnn a bouquet of colorful wild flowers. "I picked these off the side of the highway," he said.

JulieAnn laughed at that, a clear picture of him parking in the middle of the road, with people trying to pass by as he stepped into the long grass to pick flowers, ran humorously through her mind.

"Thank you. They're beautiful." She took them in her arms and buried her face in their petals, inhaling their perfume, then stepped close to him, reaching on tip-toe to kiss his cheek. They looked at each other for a moment, then she said, "Why don't you come in while I find a vase for these."

Tandon looked around while she rummaged through the cupboards. "This is a nice place you have here," he said.

"Thanks," she said. "I've been here about eight years now. It's small, but cozy. Suits my needs," she said with a shrug. "And how about you? Do you have a place you call home?"

"The Park Service puts me up at whatever location I'm at. I wouldn't bother to own a home unless I was sure I would stay there permanently."

"That makes sense," she said. "Do you have plans to do so? Stay somewhere permanent, I mean?" she asked as she put the flowers in the vase, then water.

There was a long pause before he answered, "I have been thinking about it."

She placed the vase on the table and faced him slowly. "Do you know where that would be?" she asked.

"I'm not sure yet," he told her after another pause.

A lot of questions were running through JulieAnn's mind, but she asked none of them. Now wasn't the time - for either of them.

JulieAnn looked at the clock on the wall. "Oh," she said, "we better get going." Before they headed out the door with their arms laden with gifts and dishes, JulieAnn stopped and waited until he looked at her, then she said, "I'm glad you're here."

Tandon smiled with sweet tenderness in his

eyes, "Me too."

CHAPTER TEN

From what he had seen during this past week, Tandon was not at all surprised to find that like many others in the area, the way of life for the Peterson elders had not changed with the times but had remained steadfast to the customs they were raised by. It was a choice he, himself, was unable to make, but having a great affinity for the old ways and the hard, but honest, lives people lived, he had tremendous respect and admiration for those who chose to hold onto that.

    Tandon studied the farmstead as he helped JulieAnn out of the truck and as they gathered together the food and gifts. The cedar log cabin, which was home to its builders, was small but quaint, frontier style, with a wide slanted roof. Smoke curled out of the lean, stone chimney that surfaced from its attachment to what he assumed was the same, if not similar, small wood stove within. Outside, the elders of the group were seated on their shaded porch, enjoying the sights and sounds of their beloved family as they moved about; the youngest children splashing and carrying on in the cold fresh creek beside the house and the women as they passed in and out of the house carrying bowls and platters out to the long, linen covered tables that stood in the lush grass of the front yard. One man was turning meat over a typical camp-style pit, while other younger men, along with teenagers, were over in a cleared area of the field playing baseball and commanding a lot of attention with every play. It was quite a gathering for one family, Tandon thought with a bit of envy. He wondered if, someday, he might find himself rocking on his own porch, surrounded by the love of his own family.

"Are you ready?" JulieAnn asked him, smiling encouragingly.

"Sure. Let's go," he said, smiling back. In fact, he was feeling pretty relaxed. Despite the ridiculous dream that had set him back this morning, he was now doing just fine and feeling pretty good about the rest of the day.

They had parked, with the other vehicles, outside of the fence and had to maneuver their way through to the gate. As they did so, Tandon admired the strategic layout of the buildings. The house was the first building set straight in and opposite the fence they were headed for. To their right and across the creek were the chicken shed and machine shed built back to back in a combination of log and board. Forward from them stood larger barns. Two of them. One for cattle, the other for the storage of hay and farm supplies. The only things lacking on this side of the creek were the actual animals.

He turned his attention back behind the house where there was a smokehouse that, despite looking like it had seen its last day, was still, in all likelihood, being used. And further still, and to the right, a privy. Apparently it was still being used as Tandon witnessed a man stepping out from it and a young girl running toward it. A quick look to the old hand pump on the side of the house with a jug sitting under it confirmed that they had indeed stuck with the old way. They had never gotten indoor plumbing, preferring instead to continue carrying it from springs nearby.

Then last, and farthest to their left, were the fields. They used to yield plentiful crops like wheat, corn, and vegetables, but as JulieAnn had said, they've retired the fields. Their main purpose, such as it was today, appeared to be as a playground and baseball diamond. Back behind them on the road, which they would have met if they had kept driving and which was just some yards from the farm, was the river where he swam with JulieAnn and her family back in the day.

Tandon looked at her then as they reached the gate. They smiled at one another in this, their last minute alone, before joining the group. Then Tandon pushed open the gate, cringing at the raucous sound it emitted as, together, they stepped inside.

* * *

The sound had alerted their arrival to the young boys that were now running around the yard with their wet clothes clinging to them. Their heads turned simultaneously and they yelled, "Hi, Aunt JulieAnn!"

That attracted everyone's attention, and as the boys came tearing over to them, the family, as if on cue, stopped what they were doing and made their way over. JulieAnn made the introductions while they ambled over to the house. Picking up each youngster for a hug and kiss she told Tandon, "These are Katie's boys. This little guy is Sam...this here is Timmy...and this one is Aaron. Boys, say hello to my friend, Tandon." Each child stuck their hand out for a shake and a "Hi," before racing away to more exciting adventures.

JulieAnn's sisters, along with their husbands, were the first of the adults to meet them, followed by her parents. "Tandon, this is the boys' mother, Katie and her husband, Art. But you probably remember her and most of the others."

"I do, but they're all grown up now. I think I need a refresher," he said, shaking their hands, smiling.

"I thought you might," she said enjoying herself. "This is Marie, and her husband Lucas. And of course, my parents, John and Sara."

"Well, Tandon," her father said, exchanging a hand shake, "it's been a long time. How've ya been son?"

"Fine. Just fine sir," he said.

"D'ya hear that Sara? The boy's making me old before my time." He faced Tandon, "You just call me John. Save the sir for the nursing' home."

"Yes s...John." They all laughed.

When her younger siblings reached them, she

said, "Jack, you were just a toddler when you met Tandon so you probably don't remember him."

"No, I don't," he said. "I'm Jack."

"Tandon. It's good to see you again."

"And these four you've never met," she said, pointing to each one as they stuck out their hands in greeting. "Thomas…Billy…John Jr., we just call him Junior…and little Anna."

"It's just Anna," she said playfully scrunching her nose at JulieAnn.

"Why don't I take these plates from you and you can go say hello to your grandparents," JulieAnn's mother said, shooing everyone away.

Tandon and JulieAnn walked up the steps of the porch to the waiting couple.

"Hi, Gran," JulieAnn said, bending down to kiss the soft cheek. "Happy birthday," Then she did the same for her grandfather. "Hi, Gramps."

"How's my favorite granddaughter," Frank said in his deep gruff way.

"I'm fine Gramps," then bent closer to him and lowered her voice, "but you better not let them hear you say that," she said about her sisters, winking at Tandon.

"Ah, poo," he said with a dismissive wave of his hand.

"Gran, Gramps, do you remember Tandon Bowman?"

"I seem to recall the name," her grandmother said.

"Well ya should maw, it's all we've been hear'n 'bout lately." JulieAnn looked apologetically at Tandon but he didn't seem put off by it.

"I brought him with me," she said.

"Well, where is he then?" Frank asked, leaning forward in his chair.

"He's right here," JulieAnn said.

"So watch what you say, old man," Annabelle warned.

JulieAnn pulled gently on Tandon's arm, "You'll have to get close. His eyesight is not what it used to be."

"The ol' buzzard refuses to wear his spectacles," Annabelle said, clicking her tongue.

"If I had 'em, I wouldn't be able to hear so good woman. If I had a choice, I'd rather be hear'n than see'n anyhow."

"Oh, you ol' fool."

"Ol' bat."

JulieAnn and Tandon couldn't contain their amusement and laughed. "Don't let them scare you," JulieAnn said. "These two wouldn't hurt a fly."

Frank Peterson had taken hold of Tandon's hand just then, "Not 'less that fly hurt us first," he said, giving Tandon a tight squeeze.

JulieAnn's mother stopped at the bottom of the steps, "Y'all get washed up. Supper's ready."

"I haven't seen Jess yet." JulieAnn said to her, "Do you know where he is?"

"I saw him heading down to the river earlier." Sara turned around, addressing anyone within earshot, "Anyone seen Jess lately?"

They all agreed that he had gone to the river.

Sara faced her daughter again, "Looks unanimous. Why don't you go round him up, and

Tandon, would you mind helping mom and dad down to the table?" With that settled she headed over to her husband, sweating over the pit.

"I'm sorry," JulieAnn said to Tandon, "I won't be long."

"That's alright. Take your time." Tandon said.

"Ya best not either," her grandfather said. "Ain't wise to let a man go hungry."

"It's true dear. They get more ornery than usual."

"Hush woman!"

"Hush yourself ya ol' coot!"

"Woman..." he growled.

JulieAnn turned and headed to the river, shaking her head and chuckling, hoping Tandon could survive until she got back.

* * *

Washed and starving the Peterson clan bustled around the tables, the youngsters filling their plates first, with the help of their parents, before everyone else dug in. Tandon held back, waiting for JulieAnn. She wasn't gone long before she returned with her brother, his fishing gear in hand.

Walking over to meet them, JulieAnn said, "Jess, you remember Tandon. Tandon, Jess."

"I remember him," Jess said tonelessly.

Tandon held his hand out to the other man, but instead of taking it, Jess put his arm around his sister's shoulders, a defiant look in his eye. Tandon recognized the warning right away. Jess was making it clear, quite clear, that he would not hurt his sister again. And if he did, it was her brother he would answer to. His protective attitude told

Tandon, if there was to be a relationship with JulieAnn, it would need approval by Jess to work.

After a tense moment, Jess told JulieAnn, "Tell maw I'll be right there. I have to wash up first," and he headed off.

As they joined the family, Tandon noticed that JulieAnn had a worried look which she tried masking under a facade of smiles and overly zealous interest in the variety of foods she flooded her plate with. He wanted to ask her about it, but with everyone around, it wasn't a good time.

Finally, when everyone was seated John said, "Paw, you want to give thanks?"

Frank Peterson bowed his head, the others following his lead as he began, "Thank thee dear Lord for this bounty b'fore us. Thank thee for the hands that prepared these here foods and may it nourish our bodies. We thank thee most 'specially for another year with maw and that ye find need of her here for more years to come. And finally, dear Lord, we thank thee for this home and the families represented here and we ask that ye guide us and keep us and direct us in the ways ye would have us. And we offer this prayer in your Son's most Holy Name. Amen."

"Amen," they all chorused.

Just before the prayer had ended, Tandon had looked up to find Jess staring stone-faced at him from across the table. Thankfully, the "Amen" allowed his freedom from that direct eye contact when JulieAnn lifted her eyes to him. He saw her look from him to her brother, then back again before looking down at her plate, the worried look back on her face. Something had definitely happened when she had gotten her brother and it was putting him on edge.

Conversation during the meal was light and easy going. With a family as large as this one was, there seemed to be a lot to talk about. And talk they did with many conversations going on at once. None of them seemed to notice, or mind, that they were nearly shouting as one spoke to another at the opposite end of the table, or that others were speaking diagonally and across from them or from one table to the other. There was talk of money and kids, sports and weather, jobs and the war. There was even some light ribbing going on that the recipients took in good fun, giving back as good as they got.

Tandon was laughing right along with them and joining in the conversations, but his earlier mood was gone tempered by JulieAnn, who sat to his right picking and pushing her food around her plate, and Jess, who kept eyeballing him.

When supper was over, the dishes were set on one table while the gifts for Grandmother Annabelle were piled before her and a cake was brought out of the house by JulieAnn's mother. After a "Happy Birthday" song had been sung, and cake had been handed out, the unwrapping began.

The younger boys had finger painted a picture of the family tree on a large poster board that everyone admired with real fascination. Then it was JulieAnn and her siblings' turn. They had all gotten various gifts such as a record of her favorite bluegrass music and a new housecoat with matching house shoes. One had secretly snatched their grandparents' photos and had arranged them in a handsome scrapbook while another had gotten a matching pearl necklace and bracelet set. Then there were the clip-on earrings and sweater pins.

Annabelle let out a gusty laugh, "If I didn't know better I'd say my age must be showing. You're all trying to pretty me up."

"Maybe I oughta git my specs on fur this," Frank teased his wife.

"Git on with ya," she laughed.

JulieAnn's parents handed over their gifts then - one lap rug and a matching shawl for across her shoulders that Sara had crocheted for her mother-in-law.

There was one last gift to be opened. Katie lifted it, turning it around, "There's no name on it," she said. "Who is it from?"

"That would be me," Tandon said, raising his hand slightly.

JulieAnn turned to him, surprise spread across her face, "You didn't have to do that," she said.

"Sure I did," he smiled, "it's not every day you turn seventy-five. Go ahead and open it," he said to Annabelle.

All eyes were on the gift as she carefully unwrapped the delicate tissue paper from around it. When she held it up there was a momentary hush, then JulieAnn spoke, "You remembered gran's collection?" She looked at Tandon awestruck.

"Well, what is it then?" Frank bellowed impatiently.

"It's a perfume bottle, dad," Sara said.

The Chimney Still Stands

"Another one?" he said.

"For my collection. You remember," Annabelle said.

"It's beautiful," JulieAnn said.

"It is at that," her grandmother agreed softly.

"Well, what's so great 'bout it?" Frank demanded.

Gran held it up to the sunlight, turning it this way and that, watching the light reflections.

"It's stained glass paw, like you see in church windows with a squeezable ruby-colored pump."

"Thank you Tandon," Annabelle said. "It was very thoughtful of you."

"You're quite welcome," he said.

While the women moved closer to admire each other's gifts, and Tandon's elegant and expensive looking piece, Jess was looking thunderously at Tandon. He couldn't understand why Jess was so put off when no one else seemed to be. He knew he was probably worried for his sister, and the whole issue about the river came as some concern, but they all knew that, and yet they were all treating him decently despite it. All but Jess, who seemed to be harboring his own grudge against him.

"Girls, what do you say we start cleaning up these dishes and leave the menfolk to their talk?" Sara suggested, and the women began gathering and clearing the tables before heading into the house, except for the guest of honor who had shut her eyes for a nap, her shawl and blanket wrapped cozily around her.

JulieAnn put a hand on Tandon's shoulder and looked at her brother, "We won't be long," she said, then smiled at Tandon.

Tandon watched her walk up the steps before dragging his gaze to Jess, who he knew had been watching him.

"Well, now that the womenfolk are busy and maw here's asleep, let's get down to business." John had lit a pipe and puffed on it a few times before he continued, pointing to his mark with the stem, "What have you got to say for yourself, son?"

CHAPTER ELEVEN

The atmosphere took a sudden three hundred and sixty degree turn as every eye was drawn to him, their serious expressions belying their harmonious acceptance of him only moments before.

"How do you mean?" Tandon asked, balling up the cloth napkin that lay beside his drink.

"He means, how could you have shown your face here? Don't you have any decency?"

"Jess, that's enough," John said, halting his son's outburst.

"No one here is blaming you for what's going on Tandon. You're just doing your job, and I know most of what you do is honest, commendable work. I have to wonder though, whether you truly understand the cost, for everyone, given these circumstances."

"Like you said, I'm just doing my job," Tandon said.

After a moment of puffing, John continued,

"Let me ask you Tandon, knowing the impact this change will have on so many people, do you, personally, think this plan is a good idea or not?"

Feeling cornered, and strangely hesitant to answer, Tandon moved to stand up, "I don't...I don't want to ruin your party with all this."

"You're alright there. Have a seat. The women will be out shortly with some coffee," John said waving him down. "We're just having a friendly conversation." Tandon wasn't sure he would have called it that, he thought as he settled back into his seat.

"Well, let's have it then," Frank said impatiently.

Tandon took a deep breath and squared his jaw before looking at John directly, "Yes, I believe what they are proposing is solid, and that there is substantial evidence to back that up."

"Excuses, more'n likely," Frank huffed.

"And you are willing to stand by that?" John asked.

"I am."

"Tell me something," John said. "What is it exactly that the Park Service can do for this land that the landowners can't?"

"Well, first of all, whatever they do, it can be done on a large scale. And it could be something that not all the landowners may want to do, or even have the capabilities of doing."

"Such as?"

"Regulate hunting and eliminate poaching. It wasn't long ago that the Ozarks were full of bear, elk, and bobcat, but with the lack of authority, they've been nearly wiped out. The government can reintroduce those native animals back into the region and let them reclaim their territory.

"They can also keep the forests from being logged. From what I understand, the river used to be much narrower and the water deeper, but with all the logging going on through the years, the land has gradually eroded making it wide and shallow. Fishing has decreased and pollution is rampant. You don't have to go far to see vehicles tipped in the river and trash of all kinds. When everyone owns their own section of the river it's impossible to maintain it and everyone will suffer in the long run."

"Sounds like a whole lot of hoopla to me," Jess said.

"Not at all. In fact, it's very serious," Tandon said.

"Government's trying to treat us like children is all…think'n they need to take a firm hand with us," Frank said.

"We're only trying to restore the river's innocence."

"What about our innocence?" Frank barked and startled them all by pounding his fist on the table. He rushed on, not waiting for an answer, "Why do you think folks moved out here? I'll tell you why. Our ancestors, including yours if I know my facts, craved a nourishing in their souls that weren't being fed by the slave run'n ways that drove the city folk. Those of us that come out here were simple God fear'n folk looking for a restful place to remember who we are.

"We came out to this here hill country not knowing where we was going nor where we'd end up and with nothing to call our own but the clothes on our backs. We trudged through, making our own trails, pursuing our own dreams, searching and claiming and writing our own stories. Our backs broke and our hands bled working this hard land. We lost crops and animals before learning patience and respect. And we gladly gave back to the Lord what He blessed us with.

"We lost our men to wars and our women to childbirth. We lost our old and our young to disease. And they're all buried around these here parts. You see boy, folks around here, they've earned their right to be here. And there ain't nobody fit to say otherwise. All this here effort to rid this land of its, so called, threat is nothing more than Devil's work."

"And you think I'm the 'Devil?'" Tandon said, his ire instantly aroused.

"It ain't right for no man to call another such. A man needs to know for himself what side he's on. And ye can't be having both. It's one or the other."

"What makes you all so sure you're right and the government's wrong? How do you know it's not the other way around?"

"Why…you…"

"No, Jess. It's a good question and deserves an answer," John said. "We're Christian people, Tandon. We believe in the Word of God and as such we believe God gave man dominion over the land and animals to be used as we see fit. Now yes, people do get carried away and abuse that privilege, but is it fair to take from those who use it wisely? We take what we need to survive. That includes hunting. Money is also necessary, and to have it, we need to work. Lumbering provides that money.

"There's no reason why the government can't bring in more animals if they desire or come up with a way to regulate lumbering. And do so without having to own the land. We shouldn't have to be removed from what is rightfully ours for scenery sake and animal freedom. Besides, the government already owns much of the land - rather large pieces of it I might add. And for just such purposes."

There was a pause as John took another puff on his cigar. "Tandon, do you have any idea what will happen to us if this bill passes?"

Tandon's thoughts during the past days surfaced, and knowing the risk, he answered truthfully, "I think a lot of good will happen. The area will grow..."

John let out a harsh laugh, leaning forward, "Grow? Wake up man! The government won't have to pay property taxes, or very little at that. These counties will die!"

"But there'll be tourism and new businesses..."

"So we can be hounded by outsiders three months out of the year? So we can watch backpackers and campers traipsing through our fields that we could be, that we should be, earning our living on? No. We're better off the way we are."

"Now we know how the Indians felt," Jess said with solemn sarcasm.

"I understand what you're saying, John,"

Tandon said, ignoring Jess' comment, "but I also see more than that. I see it through different eyes. That dominion you speak about does put man in charge of the land and animals. I agree. They are our life source, but they are also vulnerable. Someone has to take care of them, to protect them. In this country our government has that ability, and that right. I stand by that one hundred percent."

Tandon looked around the table to the faces watching him, "This is a big country, with plenty of room for give and take. I don't believe it's unrealistic for the government to assume the role of caretaker of what keepsakes remain."

Tandon was having a hard time controlling the urge toward anger and frustration. He had to remind himself time and again that their loss was controlling them. If they had not been personally involved, they could have stood back and seen the greater picture and understood. Bringing God into it had provoked Tandon and now he could hardly stop himself from throwing it back at them. "This country was founded on Christian values - the government leading by Godly morals. And I believe that's why we've succeeded in being the strongest nation in the world. Our laws are not unbearable or ungodly. They are justifiable."

Tandon looked directly at John when he said his next words, "Even if we disagree, God tells us, if I remember my Bible correctly, that we are to submit to governing authorities."

John met his stare, "That's right. And we do. We will. However, our own government makes it possible for us to fight it when it contradicts the very principles that are this countries foundation."

"Yes, you have that right," Tandon said.

"And we intend to use it at the House hearings."

Tandon nodded slowly, "Like some tried at the Senate hearings."

"That's right," John said.

"You know," Tandon said pointedly pausing, "the Senate passed the bill despite the effort."

"But we have one more hearing, and Lord willing, we'll succeed."

"And if you don't?" Tandon asked.

The strained silence that followed spoke volumes of the depth of sorrow and defeat they would feel.

Jess' eyes were narrow and piercing when he spoke, "You don't think we're going to win this, do you?"

Tandon was sensitive to their impending loss, but spoke the truth, "No, I don't."

"And you don't care either." Jess went on spouting his angry words growing more irate with every breath. "Why should you? You're not one of us anymore. There's no risk for you. You did your job. You did what you were told to do. No skin off your nose."

Tandon watched and listened to Jess as the intensity burned hot in his eyes, seemingly losing control for what, unexpected reason, he didn't know.

"But it's not about your job anymore is it? Sure, it may have started out that way, but it's turned into something else along the way hasn't it?"

Jess sneered as if the silent beast in him had woken. "You want something and you're here to claim it."

"I don't know what you're talking about," Tandon said and looked around at the others whose faces showed their own perplexity.

"It's a little too late to feign ignorance. You're here to do some sweet talking. Try to turn us over to your way of thinking. Trying to make it a little easier on yourself to get what you want. Why else would you have dared come here?"

"Jess," Tandon said, wanting to stop this horrible scene, but he was abruptly cut off with a curt snort.

"What a surprise it must be that you weren't able to turn even a single person to your way of thinking. You must have thought we'd be easy prey, gobbling up all your heroic efforts. Well, surprise! We weren't fooled. And you can be sure, when JulieAnn sees what a no good loser you are, she'll come to her senses and finally give you the boot you deserve."

Tandon jumped up from his seat, sloshing drinks as he bumped the table. At that same moment he saw JulieAnn standing on the porch holding a pot of coffee, her face fixed in pain. Everyone followed his gaze to the porch, including Jess, who sucked in his breath.

Immediately, JulieAnn spun around, disappearing into the house.

Art, one of the brother-in-laws, both of whom had remained silent through the entire exchange, spoke up, "Tandon, maybe it's time to take your leave."

"Jess will bring his sister home," John said, directing a severe look to his flush faced son.

"Thank you for your gift," Annabelle said, surprising them all.

"You're welcome ma'am," Tandon answered almost inaudibly, noting how alert she appeared. "Thank you for your hospitality," he added without intention.

Tandon looked toward the house wanting to say something to JulieAnn but John read his thoughts, "Leave her be. The ladies will take care of her." Tandon gave one last look toward the house, then walked to his truck and drove away, perturbed with the way things had turned out and more than disturbed by the look on JulieAnn's face.

He knew he couldn't leave things the way they were. He had to see her tonight. He had to correct any misunderstandings her brother may have planted in her mind. And he still wanted, more than anything, to tell her how he felt about her. And maybe, just maybe, if she hadn't been persuaded otherwise, he might still have a chance.

* * *

"Jul's, I've apologized a hundred times already. What more can I say?" Jess pleaded, emotionally exhausted as he drove her home.

JulieAnn had refused to speak to him. She hadn't spoken to any of her family since returning to the house after her brother's outburst. She was angry. She couldn't believe they had put Tandon on the spot like that. Especially after she had guaranteed their good behavior. She was hurt and embarrassed by their conduct.

She hadn't said anything because she didn't like confrontations of any kind, but at her brother's words she lost control. "I'm disappointed in you Jess…with all of you. How could you do that? All I asked of you was to be nice to him. You know how I feel about him. I should have listened to my instincts and left after you told me dad and Gramps were going to talk to him. But I'm really angry with you. You know better than anyone how much I still love him, but you didn't respect that. You were rude and outright hostile toward him. What came over you? I've never seen you like that."

"I don't know," Jess said, contrite. "I guess, the more I thought of it, after you invited him, the more upset I got. And before I got to Gran and Gramps' house, I had worked myself into a fit."

"Over what?"

"Come on Jul's. You're not that naïve," Jess said suddenly terse.

"Let's say that I am. Explain."

"Why do you think he came today? And bringing gran that fancy gift. Why would he go to all the trouble for someone he barely remembers?"

JulieAnn had wondered the same thing initially but passed it off as he was just being courteous.

"He has feelings for you, and they're more than just friendly. You can see it a mile away. And what of his job? How does that play into it?"

"You know so much, why don't you tell me."

"He's proved today how strongly he stands by his career. There'll be no budging. He's not an idiot, Jul's. He loves you and he knows the fate of our family's farm. He's trying to get around that by making them sweet on him so he can court you with their blessing."

"Oh, you have such a big imagination," JulieAnn said, more irritated with her brother than she ever imagined being. "In case you had forgotten, he didn't want to come in the first place, but I pushed him...regrettably. As far as his feelings go, there's never been any admission of love on his part, or mine. He's only seen me a few times since he's been here. He hardly knows me." As she spoke, she was reminded of their date and her belief that he wanted to confess his love to her.

"And how well do you really know him? All you have to go on are your memories. Most likely, he's changed since then. And what if he did tell you he loved you, you'd probably tell him the same. Then what? Say you want to get married. He's put a hundred percent into his career. He's not going to give that up. Are you willing to leave your family and travel around wherever his job takes him? Because you'll have to, you know. He's not going to settle back down here. He wanted to leave here remember? And what will our family think when you up and leave with a man who's involved in the one thing that's going to ruin their lives? You want to lose your family like he lost his?"

"They wouldn't do that to me," JulieAnn said.

"Like Gramps said to Tandon, you have to pick what side you're on. You can't have both." Jess steered his car into her driveway then and JulieAnn opened her door. "Think about it," Jess said before she slammed it shut.

Inside her bedroom, JulieAnn jerked one of her

jogging suits off its hanger. Its soft velour material was a favorite of hers, having a comforting quality about it. And now, needing that comfort, she couldn't get it on fast enough. She felt dirty and ashamed and it had nothing to do with her brother or the others...but with herself. This past week, not to mention for years, she had been so deeply involved in her own feelings that, though she was aware of the truth, she wasn't 'awake' to it. Not until that afternoon.

None of the men had seen her as she carried the coffee out of the house, and their conversation had continued. As she had moved to take a step down, her grandfather's fist pounding on the table, had stopped her. His next words, vehemently spoken, grounded her to the spot. And she remained so until Jess' guilty face urged her retreat.

Now, she realized, it wasn't her family that she was upset with, but herself. If she hadn't been so self-absorbed she would have realized the torment her family was going through.

Her painful admission was quickly draining her of energy and she made a move to lay on the bed, but there was a knock on the door. It was probably her folks coming to check on her. Assuming so, she didn't look out the window, but opened it expectantly. She couldn't have been more wrong.

Neither spoke, but looked to the other...their moods mimicking. Then Tandon asked, "Can I talk to you?"

JulieAnn stepped back pulling the door open with her. She remained that way with her hand on the door as he said softly, "I'm sorry about what happened earlier."

"I'm sorry I made you go. I shouldn't have. I didn't realize…"

"You didn't. I wanted to."

There was a painful silence that JulieAnn didn't know how to fill. She moved to sit at the table, but left the door open, unwilling to have it closed. Tandon remained standing.

"JulieAnn, I don't know how much you heard, but I don't want you to think what Jess said was true. I'm not trying to con my way into your family. I did hope, though, for a chance to talk to you alone, and tell you…"

"Why you left?" JulieAnn lifted her eyes tiredly, the question coming automatically and without forethought. She knew she was grasping at straws, that it wasn't what he wanted to talk about, but she needed to ask it…finally. "Sixteen years ago you left without a word or a call. Not even a note. You just left, with no explanation and no goodbye. Didn't I deserve some notice?" Tandon hung his head and she could see how uneasy and uncomfortable he was with her questions. She didn't care. She was ready for an answer.

Tandon cleared his throat and admitted, "I was a stupid kid, JulieAnn. I wanted things to be the way I dreamt them. And I was in a rush. I was afraid if I stayed just one minute more that I'd get sucked in and never leave. Back then I wasn't ready to commit to anything that would tie me down."

"You think I would have tied you down?" JulieAnn asked, hurt.

Tandon looked at the toes of his boots, "Not

you, specifically. There was also the farm, and...I just needed to go," he breathed.

"And that you did," she whispered to herself, but Tandon heard.

"JulieAnn, I'm sorry," Tandon pleaded for her to understand and forgive him. "I know I should have said something, at least said goodbye, but I couldn't. If I'd seen you I might have changed my mind. I know it wasn't fair to you, but I was sure you'd forget about me. And you did. You moved on with your life and your own dreams came true. But JulieAnn, I've realized something," Tandon knelt before her and took both of her hands in his, "coming back here again, it's done something to me. I missed it here, and I was a fool to try and forget this place. But more than that...I missed you, and I am an even bigger fool for trying to forget you."

JulieAnn pushed her chair back and got up, moving out of Tandon's reach. Despite the agonizing hours she had spent daydreaming about a moment like this, now that it was here, she couldn't go through with it. There was too much at risk. Too many people to get hurt if she made the wrong decision.

"JulieAnn," Tandon said, getting to his feet, "I've changed, and I'm willing to..."

"Please, Tandon," JulieAnn said, stopping him. She was sure what he was going to say, but she couldn't let him. Her brother was right. His career was important to him, and she respected that. But she couldn't let him give that up for her. He'd put everything he had into it and to allow him to put it behind him would be selfish on her part. She knew, if his feelings were anything like hers were for him, that this would be painful, but she knew it would be for the best in the long run.

"You were right," she said, struggling to keep her voice firm, "I moved on with my life. And so did you. Everything is different for both of us now. You said you've changed. Well, so have I. We're not high school kids anymore, Tandon. We can't get back what we had."

"We can start over," Tandon said, taking a step toward her, his eyes pleading with hers. "We can have something better."

"No, we can't," she said as she backed up. "It won't be better…it'll just be different. There are still too many differences separating us"

"We can work on them."

"No. It won't work," she said and knew then what she had to do.

Looking at Tandon, the man she had always loved, standing there before her, it would be so easy to step into his arms and take whatever he offered, to go on as though nothing stood in their way and live out the dream she had fantasized about for so long. It was unfair, she thought, that she had to give him up now. It was unfair that the timing and the circumstances should be the blessing that brought him back into her life, then be the very evil that would take him from her. But time was up and the fantasy was over. She couldn't let this go on any longer. It had to end, for everyone's sake.

"We had something once, a long time ago, but it's over now," she said. "I'm not in love with you anymore." She couldn't keep the quiver from her voice any longer and her legs shook. Her whole body seemed to be failing her, a testimony to the struggle within herself. "I'm sorry, Tandon." She walked to the door, holding onto it for support.

"JulieAnn, don't do this. I know that's not true. I know we can work this out. Please, give us a chance."

Tandon had moved to stand in front of her and his presence nearly made her give in, but she saw her family in her mind and her brother's words echoed through her confirming the decision she was making. "I'm sorry," she said again and looked down, unable to face him and the pain she was causing.

After a moment Tandon said, "Me too," then quietly, and slowly, turned away from her.

Her heart was shattering into pieces. She dreaded, with every thunderous beat of her heart, the moment he would step out of her house, and out of her life for good. Every second was torture. In her mind she screamed for him to go, now, before she could change her mind. Another voice, unreasonable and selfish, yelled at Tandon, "Where are you going? Fight harder. Make me change my mind. Hold me and never let me go."

She was going to crack, she knew, and she didn't want him to see it. When he finally stepped out the door, she lost control. Gulping, a painful act, she whispered, "I'm sorry," and quickly shut the door. Pressing her back against the cool wall, she breathed deeply, trying to keep from collapsing.

Then she heard Tandon, still standing just

outside the door, "I love you, JulieAnn." Her breath caught in her throat as the words she had hoped to hear sunk in. Then she heard his footsteps and reality hit her like a slap. She cried then, sinking to the floor. Details of him swam through her mind. His face, his smile. His arms and how right it felt being held in them.

Her torment was relentless. She heard his truck start and she jumped up, panic feeding her urgency and looked out the window, the lace curtain shoved open in time to see him pull away, never looking back.

After a time, she pulled herself from the door and made her way to her room. She stood in the doorway, not knowing what she should do. Her mind was quiet. No thoughts surfaced. No ideas formed. She felt hollow. With a will of their own, and without her being aware of it, her eyes were drawn to the dresser. It took some time to focus through the fog before she could see what held her attention. It was the arrowhead Tandon had given her. She walked over to the dresser and gently picked it up. She carried it to the bed and sat down, looking at the details very closely. She remembered the day he found it. Every memory of those hours spent with Tandon played like a movie in slow motion.

She cried all that night, the rock held tightly in her fist, the jagged edges digging into her skin, unnoticed, until the sun started peeking into the window. Then, she slept.

CHAPTER TWELVE

Tandon drove around Harrison, wandering aimlessly through the streets. He hadn't a destination in mind when he left the hotel - his desire was only to get out. He needed a break from his thoughts and the dizzying confines of the small room. He wasn't hungry in the least, but he found himself searching for a restaurant nonetheless. Maybe a strong cup of coffee would perk him up, not to mention, wake him up. It had been a long trying night, and he was glad it was over.

The more he yearned for that coffee the more frustrated he became. It seemed everything in town was closed. No restaurant was lit and no gas station running - his last and most dreaded option. The stores were vacant and the square downtown was silent and void of activity. The streets had only a minimum amount of activity and those he passed near enough to seemed to be dressed for a special occasion.

Of course, he thought, he was in the Bible belt. Towns were shut down on Sundays. It was a day of worship and everyone went. Tandon zigzagged through the area noting the church buildings people pulled up to. There were the Baptists, the Assemblies of God, the steepled community churches, and the Methodists. He knew very little about any of them.

He turned down another road on the edge of town, intent on heading back to the hotel. Maybe they would have some coffee on in the lobby. Stopping for a red light, Tandon was surprised to see a building he recognized. He set his blinker and at the green light turned left down a short lane, slowing to a crawl to observe the sign. It read, "The Church of Christ Meets Here."

He remembered it well, surprisingly enough. His mother had taken him as a young boy. She, herself, had gone all of her life, up until she had become too sick to travel. His father, however, had never gone - as a youth or adult - and had refused to take him - even when his mother couldn't, so Tandon hadn't been back to it, or any other, since.

Without forethought he pulled into the parking lot and again observed the sign. The worship times on the board told him the morning service had started five minutes ago. He turned off the engine and got out. It seemed his body had a mind of its own. He'd had no intention of going to church that morning, but suddenly there he was, turning the knob to the door - the rich sounds of their voices, boldly singing praises and hymns, flowed past him and out to the street.

Quietly, Tandon slid into a pew in the back where only a few had noticed his entrance and smiled warmly at him, encouraged by the new face that joined them. Taking a songbook from his seat he tried to politely peek over a shoulder, but was interrupted by a lady near him who tapped him on the arm and tipped her book to show him the page they were on.

"I'll Fly Away." Tandon recalled the song and joined in quietly at first - he could barely hear himself, then gradually louder, enjoying the peace of it. He was pleased and surprised to recognize many of the songs. They had been some of his favorites as a child. He was feeling very restful and strangely secure as he sang and was more than a little sorry when it ended. He would have liked it to continue.

Then the preacher began his lesson. The subject was entitled, "Do you know where you're headed?" Tandon was taken off guard at that. It was stupefying how accurate the question was. Its precision intimidating. Obviously, the expected assumption was regarding Heaven or Hell. But for Tandon, it posed questions about other things as well. Though in the end, he guessed, it all came down to that.

Throughout the lesson Tandon wavered between a mixture of awe and discomfort. At times, it seemed, the preacher had known he was coming and was tackling the difficulties of his life and personal demons for his benefit. And at other times he wanted, desperately, to slide down in his seat and hide as his eyes darted around to see if anyone had noticed him - his guilt. But always their eyes remained looking forward, listening, relating the lesson to their own lives - no one paying heed to him.

The preacher spoke of God as being our Creator and Father and, as such, desires much from His children. And through His love He has given the right, to every individual, to make their own decisions and choose the paths they would follow. He did not leave mankind to dangle treacherously on a limb, however, but gave examples in His Word to direct us.

The preacher also reiterated the promises God has made regarding consequences for traveling the wrong path and receiving the ultimate reward for following the righteous path. He also pointed out that at some point in a person's life, which he referred to as the "age of accountability," that one would be held responsible for one's own actions. There will be no opportunity to blame others for their choices. There will be no room for, "He made me do it," or, "That's how I was raised," because in the end each will have to give an account of themselves.

Though the lesson had been short, roughly forty minutes, Tandon had been given much food for thought. He couldn't help wondering, despite his desire to attain his dream job, had the path he chose been the wrong one?

Earlier he had felt guilty when the preacher had begun. It had been a strange sensation. Since he had left home, he had never felt guilty in the least bit, but justified. It was his life. It wasn't his responsibility to carry on for his father. Farming had been his dream. It was his father's responsibility. He shouldn't be forced into someone else's dream.

Maybe he had been wrong and now he was paying the price. No! That couldn't be, Tandon chided himself. Why should he not have the right to live his own life? Maybe he had been right. Who's to say just because you have a child that they must follow in your footsteps? He would never make a child of his a slave to his life. He would encourage him to make his own way and be proud of him no matter what. His mother had encouraged him. She had even told him to go. She understood. Guilt washed over him again then. He had told her he would make her proud.

When the service was over Tandon headed out to his father's place. He had promised himself that he would make amends and he intended to do just that. But he was worried. He wasn't sure how to get back into his father's good grace. He didn't know what would be expected of him.

All his previous confidence had gotten lost somehow and he was no longer sure about anything anymore - as if he didn't know his own mind, right from wrong or which path would lead him to the light and which to self-destruction.

He had thought he had known his direction and seen the rewards, but as of yesterday, all that had changed.

* * *

Tandon sat behind the wheel, parked before his father's house, fighting with himself over whether to stick with his plans or escape before he was seen. The temptation toward the latter was overwhelming but he opened the door, forcing himself out, willing himself to just go and get it over with and take the risk. At least he couldn't say he hadn't tried.

Slowly, Tandon walked to the house and knocked on the door. After a moment his father pulled open the door and looked at his son. Without a word he turned around, moving to his recliner, and sat, picking up his plate of food from the TV tray beside him and focused on the news report being televised before him.

Tandon had entered the house, and after an uncertain pause, took a seat in the chair his mother had favored and looked around. Everything was exactly the same. And it was clean, which surprised him. He didn't remember his father to ever pick up after himself. His had always been a consistent pattern of dropping clothes here and tools there as he passed from one room to another, leaving his wife the honor of retracing his steps to retrieve and replace the misplaced items to their proper haven.

Neither spoke as Isaac finished his meal, getting up only when the news had ended. Bringing his empty plate to the kitchen counter, he pulled a beer from the refrigerator before returning to his chair. "What do you want?" Isaac asked, staring at the TV and taking a long swig from the bottle.

Tandon wasn't sure how to go about starting the conversation so he told him his intention. "I'd like us to make amends."

"Us?"

Tandon could see his father wasn't going to

make this easy on him. "I. I would like to make amends."

"How do you plan on doing that?" Isaac asked, still not looking at his son.

"I'm not sure," Tandon said truthfully, ignoring his father's snort. "I was hoping you could help me out with that."

"You made your bed. Now lie in it." Isaac took another long drink and wiped his mouth with the back of his hand.

Tandon had to bite his cheek to keep his calm. "I have to leave tomorrow," he said.

"Good for you."

"I was hoping we could at least be on speaking terms. I'd like to keep in touch."

"Why start now?"

Good question, Tandon thought before remembering his goal. "You're the only family I have."

"You poor thing," Isaac sneered.

"And I'm the only family you have."

"That's where you're wrong," Isaac said, finally eyeing his son. "Sharing my blood doesn't make you family. You lost that right the day you quit on us. I have a new family now...my friends and neighbors. They're the ones I count on."

"I'd like us to be a family again," Tandon said.

"It's too late for that."

"I don't think so."

"Well now, I don't really care what you think. Just like you didn't care what I thought."

"Look. Maybe I was wrong then. I don't know. But I can't go back and change it, so I'd like to now."

"No," Isaac said, looking back at the television.

"Why not?"

"I told you. It's too late."

"You won't even try?" Tandon was perplexed.

"That burden is on your shoulders."

"Why do you think I'm here now?" Tandon was highly exasperated with his father's childishness.

"Your guess is as good as mine," Isaac finished off his beer and rose to get another.

Tandon stood up, following his father. "Look, alright, I'm sorry. I'm sorry for everything I've ever done. Sorry I couldn't measure up. Sorry for my stupid dreams. Sorry I didn't want what you wanted. Sorry I left."

"You forgot one," Isaac said. Seeing Tandon holding his hands out in question, he answered, "Sorry for who you turned out to be."

"Of course," Tandon said, "that too. And sorry for living if that'll make you happy. What else do you want from me?"

For all of the tension he felt, Tandon noticed quite the opposite in his father. Isaac seemed to be as calm a man as he'd ever seen. This alone was enough to aggravate Tandon to no end.

"I want you to prove it."

"How?" This he nearly shouted.

"Fix this problem."

"What do you think I'm trying to do?" Tandon was nearing the end of his rope.

"I'm not talking about us. I'm talking about this whole deal with the river. I'm talking about losing my home."

"I can't do that." His father had gone mad.

"Yes, you can."

"No, I can't. I'm only a surveyor."

"But you have connections. You can reach all the right people."

"What are you talking about?"

"Convince them they're making a mistake. Fix your reports."

"No! Are you crazy? That would be the end of my job."

"Well, we'd be a family again. You could come back and help me run the farm."

"Have you lost your mind? I can't do what you're asking. Not for any reason."

"And I can't do what you are asking." Isaac said looking pointedly at his son.

Tandon was exasperated. And mostly with himself. What was the matter with him this week? He seemed to have lost touch with reality. Really! What had he been thinking? Clearly there was just something about this place that was just…wrong. No wonder he'd had to get out of there. He would never have, and was not going to, get anywhere.

Tandon wanted to beat on something he was so unnerved. "Obviously, I have chosen the right path and I finally see the light," Tandon said heading to the door. "Thanks for clearing that up, dad," he said then abruptly turned back to his father. "You know, I actually pitied you this week. Can you believe that? But you don't need pity do you? You need help. Not to mention a heart and soul, like maw had."

Tandon left then, storming over to his truck. He heard his father say something and he turned sharply, opening his mouth for a rebuttal, then stopped. His father wasn't talking to him. Standing in the opposite direction, and not too far from him, was Jess. He watched as JulieAnn's brother turned from the hood of his father's truck, his hands black, reaching for the rag hanging from the back pocket of his overalls.

"You can tell JulieAnn I won't be needing her this week," Isaac was saying. "I've kept up pretty well since her last cleaning. Maybe the following week."

"I'll be sure to let her know," Jess said.

Isaac went back into the house then, but Tandon remained glued to the spot. He was letting that exchange sink in as Jess walked over to him.

"I guess you didn't know," Jess said seeing Tandon's expression.

"No, I didn't," Tandon said looking away.

"She's been coming by since your mother's funeral."

Tandon faced Jess, the lines between his brows deepening. "Why?"

Jess was stuffing his smeared rag back into his pocket, "I'm sure you can imagine."

He did, and the anger of only moments ago was exchanged by a deep sadness.

"She quit talking about you about then," Jess said.

Both men stood there looking out over the hillside.

"Look," Jess said, "I was out of line yesterday."

"Don't worry about it," Tandon said, then turned and opened the door emotionally drained.

"Tandon," Jess said, stopping him, "if you had to choose, between your job and JulieAnn, which would it be? No, don't answer," he added quickly as Tandon opened his mouth, "just think about it. And if it's your job you choose, then let her know so she can get on with the rest of her life."

Tandon turned the key in the ignition as Jess returned to his father's truck, the other man's words replaying in his mind. "Too late, Jess," he said to himself, "she's already made that decision." He headed out then, away from his home, away from his love, his desire, and away from his nightmare. It was over.

* * *

It was seven o'clock when Jess left her. He had stopped in to check on her and had stayed for dinner and a chat. He had told her everything. Tandon's visit with Isaac. About Tandon's surprise to learn she had been taking care of his father. Jess had even told her what he had said to Tandon. Now, as she stood at the counter drying their dishes, she couldn't help but feel a sense of urgency. Her heart was racing despite her attempts to be logical. She knew she shouldn't expect Tandon to call her. After all, she had been the one to end it. It was she that had made the final decision for both of them, so why should she expect him to come running back to her. It was foolishness, she knew, but felt it in her heart, that if he was willing to give up his job for her, she would accept that gladly and never look back. On one hand, she didn't expect him to come, but on the other, he loved her. She'd heard him say it. So maybe, just maybe…

There was a knock on the door and she jumped. Quickly she pulled the apron from her waist, patted her hair anxiously, and took a deep breath before stepping to the door to pull it open.

"Hi, JulieAnn." Rebecca stood on the porch holding Daniels hand.

"Oh. Hi," JulieAnn said, looking at their beaming faces while hers melted.

"Are you busy? Daniel wants to see the new movie that's playing in town so we thought we'd see if you wanted to join us."

"Ah…" JulieAnn looked at Daniel who was hopping up and down, clearly excited.

"Yeah, come on JulieAnn, it's gunna be funny," he said.

"What do you think?" Rebecca asked.

"I can't," she breathed, "not tonight."

Rebecca was looking curiously at her, but Daniel remained nonplussed.

"Is everything okay?" Rebecca asked.

"Yeah, fine. Everything's fine Becca." Then she turned to Daniel to take the attention off of herself, "But you have lots of fun Daniel okay, and you can tell me all about it tomorrow."

"Okay. Come on mommy, wur gunna be late."

Rebecca grinned at her son then looked at JulieAnn. "I guess I'll see you tomorrow then."

"Okay. Bye."

After waving to Daniel, JulieAnn closed the door. Her mood had been severely dampened by her disappointment. She was just kidding herself, she knew, but maybe she should call him. He was probably just afraid to approach her after how she had treated him. Her spirits rose as she considered this. If she apologized, maybe...well, she ought to anyway. It didn't guarantee anything would change, though, and she knew this. Yes, she understood it, but how would she know otherwise.

JulieAnn had made up her mind to call, but the next problem was to rehearse what she planned to say. After working it all out she looked at the clock. It was twenty after eight. Quickly, before she could change her mind, she looked in the phone book for the number to the hotel then lifted the receiver. As the dial tone sounded her mind went blank. She'd forgotten what to say and quickly hung up. She went over it again, saying it out loud, then dialed again.

A woman with a sing-song voice answered, "Good evening, Holiday Inn, how may I help you?"

"Hi," JulieAnn said and had to clear her throat, "could you connect me to Mr. Bowman's room please? Tandon Bowman."

"One minute, please."

JulieAnn closed her eyes, waiting for a masculine response, but was disappointed when the cheery feminine one returned.

"I'm sorry, ma'am. That gentleman has already checked out. Said he couldn't wait to get home. A very likeable man I must say - and a very handsome ma..."

"Thank you," JulieAnn interrupted and hung up.

Walking into the living room, she moved to sit

gently upon her loveseat. Pulling her legs up, she crossed them onto the cushion, and with her hands in her lap, she began to rock, slowly, back and forth. There was nothing left to hope for - nothing left to dream. It was over.

CHAPTER THIRTEEN

PRESENT

Tandon twisted the cap off of his second medicine bottle and tilted it, letting one pill slide into his palm to join the other. Placing them on his tongue, he put the canteen to his lips and tipped his head, swallowing, desperate for the small measure of relief that would soon follow. Leaning his back against the rock he waited.

It was only mid-morning but Tandon could already feel the sun's warmth easing the chill from his body. The orange glow he had seen in the sky the previous evening, as he reached his childhood home, had held the promise of a beautiful day to come. And he was not to be disappointed.

Tandon shifted his weight. He was moving cautiously, his entire body aching. Whether he was sore from yesterday's long hike up the road, made even more strenuous by the load he carried, the cold hard ground he had slept on, or simply the life hindering symptoms of his disease, he didn't know. But he was determined to not let it interfere with his goal. He had to remain focused. There were but a few days left, as recent experience had shown, before the relieving effect of his latest transfusion would wear off. Then he would need to be home.

Achieving a certain level of comfort, Tandon rose slowly to his feet. Pausing for a moment to allow his body to adjust, he looked again to the remains before him. Inexplicably drawn to it, he had hardly taken his eyes from it since first seeing it last night, then again waking to its presence this morning. With the contorting shadows of the sunset and sunrise the scene had appeared sad and unkempt, but now, with the sun high in the sky, it became less forlorn and more like an artifact or monument.

That made him smile. The idea that someone might see this as anything other than the dilapidated ruin it was was ludicrous and far-reaching at best, but it was there - the beauty in the rubble. And Tandon studied it, though with the trained eye of one whose life's work was centered around the past, whose mind envisioned every detail of every sound, every word, and every movement. This time, however, there would be no romanticizing for he knew the story.

Tandon moved to where he had slept the night before. It was the exact spot he had slept in every day of his life, up until the time he had left. It had been easy enough to find. Though the majority of the house had been torn down and removed, the foundation was still there lending him the guide by which he followed. And if that had not been enough, there remained another feature - the chimney.

Tandon had been pleasantly surprised the night before when he finally reached the end of the drive and saw the welcoming beacon towering before him. It stood tall, looking out of place where it rose from the overgrowth of grass and weeds and with vines twisting and tangling about it clinging to every pore and crevice. Much of the chimney's inner layer of rock had crumbled to the ground and lay in a sprawling heap. Some of it was still blackened from the staining smoke of long ago and others were lightened by the constant abuse of weather. He had seen the remnants of homes left in such conditions many times, but never of one he had known so intimately. And strangely enough, he was not upset by it as he might have thought, but rather, he felt an overwhelming sense of peace.

On a whim, Tandon bent down and rifled through his bag for the knife he had brought. He had no intentions of using it when he had packed it, but had done so out of habit and was now glad he had as he walked carefully to the pillar and began cutting loose its thick cover.

As he worked he recalled one cool evening as his mother knitted in her chair, that he, sitting on the floor before the crackling fire playing some sort of game by himself, was interrupted by his father who had come into the room with an arm extended, then handed him an old shoe box.

Tandon smiled at the memory of opening it and

finding two wooden derby cars his father had hand carved for him along with various bottles of paint and one brush for him to decorate them with as he wished. The happy surprise had been felt by both he and his mother and had continued the whole week as each night father and son would crawl on all fours and race one another around the room.

* * *

A little over an hour had passed before Tandon finished. The sun had risen high in the sky, the air had become noticeably warmer, and he was exhausted from his work, but when he stood back and looked at the results, he felt a sense of accomplishment. Desiring to clear away the pile of cuttings he had created, Tandon bent down, scooping up an armload and as he stood a splash of color caught his attention. Using his foot, he gingerly brushed aside the remaining debris exposing, to his great surprise, the bright yellow of daffodil buds only now beginning to open. He couldn't have been more surprised. Bending down to touch one he marveled about the longevity of these visually delicate but physically hardy plants. After all these years, from his mother's first planting of them through dozens of late frosts and years of certain neglect when weeds and vines would have choked the life of any other plant, these flourished, unwilling to be denied life.

Sighing softly, Tandon stood, and walking over to a stand of trees, dropped his load. Turning then, he faced the open expanse of fields which reached the not too distant hills, and they in turn, the mountains. The view was breathtaking. A soft breeze blew up and he instinctively closed his eyes, taking it in in a slow breath through his nostrils, filling his lungs. The air smelled of new growth and warmed earth. Life. Nature beginning to waken from its winter slumber.

Tandon would have loved to stay this way, his mind free of all thought, just living in the moment, but he couldn't. The day was slipping by and he still had unfinished business to tend to. He had thought much on the walk yesterday, and some before the campfire, but today, it seemed, he had lagged about.

Walking over to the chimney, he sat, leaning against it, the view before him. He could put it off no longer, and as the memories flooded back so too did the realization that, whether good or bad, he had made the right decision in coming back.

CHAPTER FOURTEEN

SUMMER 1971

Tandon made sure to include the day's date, August 29, 1971, then turned off the typewriter and leaned back against the sofa cushion satisfied. He had to admit, he was a bit surprised at how good he felt. If someone had told him, years ago, that one day he would be making this decision he would have laughed it off and thought them crazy. Yet here he was, changing the course, steering away from everything he knew to head off into the unknown. And that was okay. The proof was in the pudding, as they say. Since making his decision the nightmares had stopped and the tension that had increasingly bore down upon him was lifted. He couldn't even recall the last time he had felt this free.

Tandon's mood slipped then as it always did when he was reminded of the circumstances that had brought him to this moment. It had been nearly a year and a half since he had returned from Arkansas, and from the moment his duties resumed Tandon's life began to spin out of control. Always a man of high standards and impeccable work ethics, Tandon redoubled those efforts, but his strategy was of the grueling, misguided, sort. And not only did he demand more of himself, but of his team as well.

Attacking his own duties with a kind of obsessive compulsiveness, he kept the work load hard and constant, bringing a certain strain to the group as their energy and efforts were depleted. Talk was soon circulating among the group regarding their boss' mental state: his short temper and how often it was unwarranted, his demand for perfection, and for those who knew him well, or not, an unsettling sense that he was on the brink of self-destruction.

Tandon himself noticed none of this as the days and weeks and months passed by. He was unaware of the dark circles shadowing his eyes and the clothes that hung loosely over the body that thinned. His world had become dominated by work, order, and routine. He spared no time for rest or fun and certainly allowed himself no time for thought. Such a punishing pace could only last so long, however, and for Tandon it took one particularly bad day, one week ago, to open his eyes to the miserable state he was in.

He had only been asleep for a couple of hours when he woke with a start, late for work. Arriving at the site he noticed the men standing around, drinking coffee and laughing over what he assumed were lewd jokes. Already in a foul mood, he lit into them. "Why are you just standing around here like you're on vacation? When you're on the clock, you work. If you don't want to work, go home."

"Sir..." one man tried to speak for the group.

"I thought I gave orders yesterday of what needed to be done today. Get your gear and move!"

"Excuse me sir," Tandon glowered at the man, but let him speak. "You told us to wait for you this morning - that there was an additional set of plans you had to bring over." He knew the man was right. He remembered setting them on the table by the door so he wouldn't forget. He shook his head, huffing disgustedly.

Growing more irate by the moment Tandon tried to think of what to do - what the men should do while he went back, because they sure as heck weren't going to waste any more time doing nothing.

Unfortunately then, one of the newer guys, always quick with a smart comment, mumbled, cursing him. He wasn't quiet enough, though, because Tandon heard him, and in the next second, having abandoned what self-control was left, he was lunging at him. Landing on top of him, he slammed his fists into the other man's face. Dust flew up from the gravel as the two scuffled, grunting with their efforts. The other men were quick to break it up, separating them physically, holding them tight as they fought to keep up the attack.

"Alright! Let me go!" Tandon ordered, jerking his arms free. After giving the other a scathing look he stalked off a short distance to catch his breath.

As he calmed down and the pain in his knuckles, and body in general, became more pronounced, the realization of what just happened pierced him. Closing his eyes, he whispered hoarsely, "Oh my God, what am I doing?" and covered his face with his hands. Even before he turned to face his crew, Tandon knew what he had to do.

Pulling the last sheet from the typewriter, Tandon picked up his pen and signed his name to his resignation. He stood up, then, grabbed his sport coat off the chair and headed out the door, ready to put an end to the charade.

* * *

Tandon stepped off the elevator and headed down the hall to see Greg Zimmerman. He was sure it would come as a shock to him, but it had to be done. He wasn't doing anyone any favors like this.

Tandon's knock on the door was answered with a curt, "Come in." Holding the phone to his ear Greg looked up and waggled his finger signaling Tandon to take a seat. While he waited Tandon looked at Greg's family photos interspersed along the shelves not far from him.

When he turned back, he noticed Greg had finished his call and was studying him and the papers he held. "Greg," Tandon began, but his boss' raised hand halted him.

"How are you doing, Tandon?" Greg asked.

"I'm fine, sir."

Greg rubbed a hand over his chin. After a thoughtful moment he asked, "So, tell me, what brings you by?"

Tandon leaned forward placing the papers on

the desk before Greg. "I'm handing in my resignation. And before you try talking me out of it, I want you to know I've thought long and hard about it. It's what I need to do."

Greg picked up the sheets and glanced through them. After a moment he set them down and lifted his head. His expression sober, he said, "Well then, I guess that's that."

Tandon's face went blank. "You're not...going to try to talk me out of it then?"

Greg smiled tiredly, "Why? It sounds as if you've already made up your mind."

"Yes. I have."

After a pause Greg admitted, "I guess I'm not that surprised. It was obvious when you got back that things had changed for you. I've never known you to be so quiet and aloof. Disturbed, I guess, would be the right word. Then when you said you wouldn't be taking that superintendent position, despite how excited you'd been, I knew something was up."

"I guess I just don't see things the way I used to," Tandon said.

"Tandon," Greg's tone became serious, "where politics is concerned someone is bound to get hurt. You can't let it get personal."

Tandon returned the look and said, "Too late."

Silence filled the room.

Finally, Greg stood and said, "Well Tandon," and stretched out his hand, "it's been an honor working with you. I wish you the best."

Tandon clasped his hand, "You too, sir," then turned away.

"I'll see to it your statement and reports are submitted at the hearing."

"Thank you."

As Tandon reached for the door knob Greg asked, "What will you do now?"

Tandon smiled, "Take a much needed vacation. As for a job," he shrugged, "I don't know yet."

"You'll always have a place here if you change your mind."

Tandon only smiled.

After he left, Greg picked up Tandon's resignation, and on a whim, instead of following proper protocol, he put it in his drawer, then opened Tandon's file and made a note he hoped would stand.

* * *

Jess Peterson had arrived at the Baltimore Washington International Airport in Maryland hours ago, and after picking up his rental car, had made his way west to Columbia. Now, circling the block for his third time, he tried to get up the nerve to complete the task he'd set out to do. Never in his wildest dreams would he have imagined he'd be doing this. And for the umpteenth time he hoped he was making the right decision.

Coming upon the Grandview Apartment complex Jess slowed to a crawl stopping, this time, in front of it and before he could change his mind, stepped out and headed up the walkway. Entering the building's first set of glass doors posed no problem, but when he tried the next set he found they were locked. Security. He hadn't thought of that. He'd have to be buzzed in. But what if, once he announced himself, he was sent away. Great. He would have come all this way for nothing.

Well, he wasn't leaving here without at least trying. Perusing the list of names with his finger, he stopped at number 208A, and before he could think about it, he pressed the call button. After a moment he heard an answering voice, "Yes?"

"Hi. I wonder if I could talk to you."

"Who is this?"

He took a deep breath. "Jess Peterson." He heard nothing for a long moment and wondered if that would be it. He pressed the button again, "It's important." He was just about to give up and leave when he heard the buzz of the door and the latch unlocking. Quickly he grabbed the handle and pulled it open then heard the words, "Second floor," spoken before the door shut behind him.

Jess took the elevator up one flight, then turned left following the arrow's direction for the first ten apartments. When he found the door with the gold numbered plate beside it he stopped. There was no turning back now. What he was about to do was risky, but it was a gamble he had to take.

Releasing his held breath Jess ran his sweaty palms over his hips, straightened his back, and raised his hand to the door. "God help me," he said, then knocked.

CHAPTER FIFTEEN

"This meeting is adjourned." With the pounding of the gavel the two hour town meeting came to its conclusion. It had been decided years ago, when all the controversy began, that the nationalizing of the Buffalo River would not go down without a fight and so, mimicking the example set by those at the 1969 Senate hearings, the heat would again be turned up.

Eight months ago, due to the landowners and sympathizers expressed concerns for what was to come and what needed to be done, meetings took place in every town along the river to discuss the issue and plan a course of action. It was determined then, by all involved, that a bus would again be sent to Washington D.C. and aboard it, to speak on behalf of those citizens left behind, there would be a group of at least fifteen strong, capable, and informed individuals who would speak out about the important issues plaguing this proposal. With the collaboration of the four conjoined counties involved, the search for those individuals began.

Now, finishing up with last minute notes, JulieAnn couldn't help but smile. The excitement in the room was contagious. The afternoon meeting had come mid-September...only six weeks before the hearing, and it had come with hope.

All who were present learned the names of those who would represent them. They learned who they were, what their occupation was, and how this proposal affected them. They also learned their reason for participating, and most importantly, what they planned to speak about. Optimism was in the air.

With an ear tuned for information, JulieAnn listened to the crowd as they sauntered about her resonating similar sentiments.

"Did you hear the names on that list?" one asked in awe.

Another answered, "Surely this is a blessing from God. Our prayers are being answered."

"Once Congress sees the full impact of what that bill promises they'll have no choice but to deny it's passing," one man said.

"I say, when this is all over, we have the biggest celebration this country's ever seen!" Others cheered and joined in, "With fireworks and parades... live music... barbecues...crawdads..."

It would be a celebration indeed JulieAnn thought, chuckling. Placing her reporting tools back in her bag, she stood up and moved to join Rebecca and her brother, Marshall Hudson.

Marshall turned to her when she reached them

and asked, "All finished?"

"Yes," she said.

"I have to say I'm getting quite excited about the whole thing," Marshall said, clearly caught up in the spirit of the moment. "I can't wait to see how this works, and how it ends, of course."

"Well, I can't see how any decent person could turn people out of their homes for what's really no good reason at all." Rebecca said. "It'll never happen."

"Let's hope you're right," JulieAnn said and smiled.

"With all this talk about food I've become quite famished. What do you say we go back to my place for dinner?" Marshall asked.

Rebecca answered quickly, "Thanks, but I've promised Daniel and Collin my undivided attention tonight." Looking directly at JulieAnn, Rebecca gave her an innocent, wide-eyed look, "But you should go, JulieAnn."

Rebecca hurriedly slung her purse strap over her shoulder and started to turn, "As a matter of fact, I'm running late. You two have fun. Save me some leftovers." In an instant she was gone, leaving the two standing alone and awkward.

Marshall laughed, embarrassed, "She's pretty obvious, isn't she?"

JulieAnn felt the heat rise to her cheeks and quickly looked down at her feet.

"The invitation's still open. I've got some steaks we can throw on the grill. They're already marinated." Marshall bent over trying to get a peek into her eyes.

JulieAnn looked up and saw his piercing blue eyes smiling at her, his eyebrows raised, cautiously questioning. It was becoming increasingly difficult to turn down Marshall's invitations. She knew if she kept it up that he would soon give up on her. She didn't like the thought of that, yet neither was she ready to take that first step of answering with a simple, "Yes."

Timidly, JulieAnn looked at him, "I'd really like to, but…"

While JulieAnn was at a loss for an honest excuse, Marshall saved her. "It's alright. I understand. Maybe when Becca's along, then," he offered, giving her an out.

"That would be great," she said relieved.

There was another awkward moment before she said, "I'll get going then."

"Let me at least drive you home," Marshall said.

JulieAnn was hesitant to insult him by turning him down again and over a very simple and safe offer, though unnecessary. She only lived a few blocks away. "I'd appreciate that," she said simply and saw Marshall's pleased smile.

JulieAnn had liked Marshall from the moment Rebecca had introduced them. He came across as being very personable and very genuine. "That's why you get along so great. You have similar personalities," Rebecca had explained.

Marshall was a year younger than JulieAnn with lots of boyish qualities that she found irresistible. His easy laugh and abundance of energy. His love of kids, as she had seen when he and Daniel were together, and always, his good natured heart. He'd surprised her the very day they'd met by unabashedly hugging her and it was something she'd come to expect and look forward to whenever they met and parted company. Like his sister, he was a native of Kansas, but while Rebecca had moved to Arkansas, Marshall had stayed behind with their parents. As their parents began traveling in their retirement years Marshall had been left most of the time without family. Missing that bond, he had come to visit his sister who had taken him anywhere and everywhere trying to convince him to move here. Finally, less than a year ago, he packed his things and made the move staying with Rebecca and her family until, getting a job working for the county road department, he was able to buy his own home.

Right away JulieAnn found herself being invited to picnics and movies, camping trips and vacations, many of which she turned down not wanting to butt into their family time. It was only recently that JulieAnn realized what was going on. Once again, Rebecca was trying to set her up. JulieAnn had never outright confronted Rebecca about it, but she was sure that that was what was going on. Oddly enough, she liked it, yet she was gun shy.

Like a gentleman, when Marshall pulled up in front of her house, he went around the car to help her out. Because JulieAnn felt bad for turning him down earlier, she offered, "Do you want to come in a minute. I made two apple pies and I just know one will go to waste before I can eat it. Will you take it?"

She could tell by the twinkle in his eye that he didn't believe her, but said, "Sure. I'm not one to pass up homemade pie."

JulieAnn smiled, "Come on in while I get it."

Neither of them heard the truck pull into the driveway as JulieAnn handed Marshall a covered dish. "Wow, that smells delicious," he said, lifting the pie to his face.

JulieAnn smiled, "It is. I promise," and giggled.

She led the way onto the porch then, and was returning Marshall's parting hug when she saw Jess walking up. "Hi!" she said, happy to see her brother.

"Hey Jul's," he returned.

JulieAnn stepped off the porch to hug Jess then turned to Marshall. "I was pawning off one of my pies on Marshall."

"You won't be sorry," Jess shook Marshall's hand. "She's the best baker around."

"I guess I'll find out soon enough," Marshall smiled. "I'll be off now. Thanks for the pie, JulieAnn. See you soon." The last he addressed to both.

After waving Marshall off the two went into the house. "How was your vacation?" JulieAnn asked.

"Ah, good. Um, Jul's…can you talk or are you busy?"

"I can talk. Want a drink?"

"No, thanks. Why don't you sit down."

JulieAnn noticed for the first time the hesitation in his words, and seeing the seriousness on his face, she grew worried. "What's wrong? Are you okay?"

Jess looked blankly at her for a moment then recovered, "Oh…yeah. I'm fine. This isn't about me."

JulieAnn was confused. "What is it then?"

Uncomfortable now that the final moment was here, Jess' mouth went dry. "Maybe I'll take that drink after all," he said and stood up.

When he returned to the table, he struggled to meet her eyes. This was it. He'd done well up to this point. Now he would see if it was all in vain…or not.

Jess looked up at his sister then and told her the truth, "Jul's, I didn't go on vacation." His heart hammered against his chest, "I went to Maryland. I went to see Tandon."

* * *

Tandon stepped out of the truck despite Jess' request for him to wait there. He couldn't help himself. He was antsy. Silently, he walked up the porch steps being careful to remain hidden from view. Jess had said he needed time to talk to his sister before she saw him and he'd agreed.

Concealing himself near the screen door, he overheard them. For the moment Tandon ignored JulieAnn's surprised reaction because it was the sound of her voice that struck him most making him catch his breath. Tandon closed his eyes, listening. It had been so long since he'd seen her, or heard her. It felt like a lifetime ago. The past year and a half had been wrought with a variety of thoughts and feelings, the worst of which was that he would never see JulieAnn again. Then, two weeks ago, while trying to decide what to do with the rest of his life, Tandon had received an unexpected visit from Jess that would provide the opportunity to change all that.

It had taken Tandon the entire first week to consider Jess' words. A week full of weighing consequences. The list was numerous on the side of good, but on the bad there was only one. Failure. Did he want to risk it? A second time? For Tandon this question was crucial. It was a state he was recently, currently, if he was being honest with himself, in and he knew he was not handling it well. In the end, he decided to go back. He would rather take the chance and know with certainty than to turn away and wonder what might have been.

The next week was spent packing and making flight arrangements. He had to dip into his savings for living expenses. Hotels were not cheap and he didn't know how long he'd be there. Regardless of how this ended, he knew he'd be looking for a job soon.

Tandon had arrived in town last night staying in the same Holiday Inn as before. After settling himself in, as much as he could under these unsettling circumstances, he had called Jess as planned. From the time Jess had picked him up this afternoon until now, standing outside of JulieAnn's door, his stomach had been aching from nervousness. Now, hearing JulieAnn's angry voice, Tandon followed the conversation.

* * *

"You had no business going to see him!" JulieAnn yelled, instantly angry and astonished that

Jess would do such a thing.

"I expected you to be upset at first, but you have to listen to me," Jess pleaded, now a bit scared of what he'd started.

JulieAnn was on her feet now thoroughly agitated. "I can't believe this. I trusted you. I told you things in confidence."

"And I haven't betrayed that. I've never told him anything you've told me," he said vehemently.

"Then what did you tell him…because it'd have to be pretty darn good for you to go all the way to Maryland to talk to him."

"I only told him what was obvious to everyone," Jess answered.

"Obvious to everyone?" JulieAnn threw her arms up, "What is so obvious to everyone that my brother thinks he can stick his nose where it doesn't belong? Let me tell you something, my life is none of your business," she said pointing her finger at him.

Jess' temper flared at that. "Is that so? Well, let me tell you something, you make it my business every time you come crying on my shoulder."

JulieAnn flipped her hair back with her hand, "I can fix that!"

"Did I do the right thing? Maybe I made a mistake," he mimicked.

"Believe me, it'll never happen again!"

"Good!" Jess said, though knowing he didn't mean it.

Walking toward her, he said, "For crying out loud Jul's, you had a chance with him. You said so yourself. He said he wanted to try. You even heard him say he loved you. But you let him go."

"I've already explained to you why," she said. "And you're one to talk! If it wasn't for your little after dinner 'man time', or should I say attack, none of it would have happened and I'd be with him right now."

"Like you, I've already explained that. The point is, I don't go around moping about it."

"I do not mope! As a matter of fact, I've been doing just fine lately. I've even decided to put the past in the past. I'm moving on. And, I'll have you know, I may be interested in someone else," she said with a smug look happy to catch her brother off guard.

It worked. Jess was speechless as he let that sink in. Then he remembered seeing her earlier as he'd walked up.

Scrunching up his face he said, "Marshall? He's not your type."

"He most certainly is. Even Becca thinks so."

"Becca," he stressed her name, "like me, would do or say just about anything to see you happy again."

"She wouldn't stoop to your underhanded methods, that's for sure."

"She already has if she's setting you up with her brother," he said in a low voice.

"Don't you dare say anything against her. Or him for that matter. He's the nicest man I've ever met and you know it. He's everything I've ever wanted."

"Really! Then why aren't you dating him? As attractive as you are and having the personality you have, I can't imagine that he hasn't asked you out."

"He has."

"Then why haven't you said yes?"

"How do you know I haven't?"

"Because I know you," Jess said. "You talk a good game, but it's all hot air."

JulieAnn huffed growing tired of it all and brought the conversation back to its original subject. "Why did you go see him?"

"I wanted to fix the sullen mood I 'perceived' you to be in." He shrugged, "I wanted to help."

"How was talking to Tandon supposed to help me?" JulieAnn asked.

Here goes nothing Jess thought. Taking a deep breath he let the words spill out, "I didn't go just to talk to him."

JulieAnn looked at Jess, waiting for him to explain.

Just then the screen door opened and at the sound both JulieAnn and Jess turned.

"He came to bring me back...to you," Tandon said.

JulieAnn, taken aback, could only gape, slack jawed, as Jess, who had turned hesitantly back to her, and Tandon, who stood silently now in the doorway, watched and waited for her to do or say something. The shock of seeing him there and the frustration from her conversation with her brother unnerved her in such a way that tears sprang to her eyes. Feeling cornered and helpless, JulieAnn, having said not one word, reached for her car keys and headed out the door behind her. Scrambling to put the key into the ignition, she noticed her brother's truck was parked behind her, blocking her escape. She didn't let that stop her, however, as she shifted the gear into reverse and backed out, right over the lawn, narrowly missing Jess' truck. Without a thought for where she'd go, JulieAnn turned onto the highway, and with tears streaming down her face, headed out of town.

CHAPTER SIXTEEN

Neither Tandon nor Jess had expected JulieAnn's reaction. Surprise? Definitely. Anger? Most likely. Happiness? They could only hope. But her silent departure? Somehow this was worse than any other reaction they might have expected. Both men had remained in the kitchen, still and silent and at a loss, as the low rumble of her car's accelerated engine faded quickly into the distance. It was only then that Tandon realized his opportunity was slipping by and made a split-second decision.

"Jess?"

Understanding immediately, Jess tossed Tandon the keys to his truck. "Don't lose her," he said.

Tandon smiled, thinking about the conversation he'd overheard. "I don't intend to," he answered, his meaning twofold. Then, with adrenaline fueling him, Tandon turned and flew out the door. Jumping down the porch steps, he ran to the truck and within seconds was racing the clock. There was no time to spare. He'd already lost precious time.

At the town square, Tandon slowed, creeping forward as vehicles before him, one after another, turned off right or left, each doing their own thing, blissfully ignorant of the mission driven man behind them. While waiting, his eyes devoured every store front, every turn off looking for JulieAnn. Right now it was a guessing game where she was and sitting there was not helping him any.

"For crying out loud," he growled under his breath barely restraining himself from blaring the horn. Impatiently, Tandon looked again at the watch Jess had left lying in the ashtray. Two minutes had passed. He snorted, hitting the heel of his hand on the steering wheel. "Come on, people." The next instant he was moving again making his way out of the small town of Jasper to head north. Or was he?

He had to think fast. Up ahead there would be four different possibilities, if indeed she had gone this way. Which one? Which one? There was the first turn off to the right, which would bring him to Hasty. Then there was a road to the left, which would immediately branch off into two others, one leading to Parthenon, the other to Ponca. He could just go straight, of course, and head into Harrison. "Why didn't I leave sooner?" he mumbled, frustrated.

Wishing there weren't cars behind him so he could think about it more he missed the first turn off to the right. Just as he was about to drive over the bridge that crossed the Little Buffalo River where he'd have to make his final decision regarding which of the other three roads to take, he saw a glint to his right. He looked. The sun had reflected off of a car winding along a dirt road that followed the river. He got a glimpse of it now and then through the trees saw the dust rise in its wake. Like a moth to a light his eyes followed it. The red '69 Ford Torino. That was it! Tandon whooped. Unbelievable! He didn't want to admit it, but he'd had his doubts of finding her. Quickly he turned around, snapped his left blinker on, turned onto the road leading to Hasty and floored it.

JulieAnn didn't know he was looking for her, he was sure, so she would, he assumed, be driving at a normal pace giving him the chance to catch up. So he thought. Curve after curve Tandon drove along expecting that at any time he would see her. That she would be just ahead. But all he saw, the only evidence of her passage, was the settling trail of dust. Perhaps she had seen him. Well, he wasn't about to give up. He knew if he could just get to her, if they could just talk...

Granted, some of the things he'd heard Jess and JulieAnn talk about had surprised him. That she'd heard him confess his love was one. He hadn't known she was listening. But even more shocking than that was hearing about her interest in another man. That had hurt. Marshall. Was that the man he had seen her hug on the porch? Even from his view, hidden as he was in Jess' truck, the guy had seemed likeable enough, but when she had talked about him his opinion had changed. He felt instant hatred toward the other man - had thought irrational and unjustifiable thoughts. But just as quickly as they came, they were gone.

Jess' continued confrontation with his sister had revealed an even greater fact. JulieAnn wasn't over him. As much as she might want to, she couldn't move on. And as long as a part of her hesitated, if for only a moment, then at least he would have a chance. If only he could catch up with her.

* * *

JulieAnn blinked rapidly trying, unsuccessfully, to clear her vision from the torrential downpour that continued to blind her. Assisting her was an already drenched hand that with each swipe across her face did next to nothing, becoming ineffectual as another onslaught of emotions spilled forth.

Despite her inability to focus clearly on the road ahead JulieAnn, distraught, kept her foot firmly pressed on the gas pedal. She couldn't run fast enough. She felt betrayed. Betrayed by a brother who, until recently, had been her confidant, her support, her protector. She thought he'd understood why she'd had to end it. She thought he had even agreed. Yes, she remembered him saying so. Then why had he gone to Maryland? Actually, the important question was - why would he bring Tandon back? On the heels of that question came another more surprising one. Why did she care? Why react with such emotion if, as she had professed to Jess, she was getting on with her life, that the past was over with? She saw his face then, standing in her doorway, his sudden appearance like that of a dream. And what she saw went beyond his physical appearance. It was his inner beauty, his strength, his vulnerability she saw. And it scared her.

JulieAnn had stopped crying at some point she was not even aware of. No longer blinded by her tears but by her train of thought alone, she had driven as if semiconscious, unaware of the direction she had taken nor of the left turn she had just made that took her off of the main road. What was clear to her was the realization that she had only been fooling herself. She was still in love with Tandon.

Without warning JulieAnn was brought to her senses by a sudden spray of water in her face. It was so cold she sucked in her breath, surprise and fear gripping her as she turned her head, looking left then right. She was in the river! Instinctively she slammed on the brakes. That turned out to be a big mistake as the rear of the car fishtailed and she continued to move forward sliding until the front right tire made a sudden dip. She let out a scream just as it came back up, righting itself before finally stopping. JulieAnn's foot was still on the brake as she maneuvered herself for a good look, the car rocking with the effort. She gasped.

* * *

Tandon continued driving down the road growing more concerned by the minute. He'd still not been able to spot JulieAnn's car since that first bit of luck in town, and now even the trail of dust had disappeared. There was no sign of her anywhere.

When he reached the next intersecting road, he looked in both directions. He didn't see her. He even looked on the ground for tire tracks and found nothing to suggest she'd been there. Tandon remembered seeing a turn off back some distance ago, but had dismissed it then. Now, left with no other alternative, he turned around.

Earlier, after turning onto the road leading to Hasty, a road which followed the path of the Little Buffalo River, Tandon had looked over to it and seen evidence of its recent flooding. The lush, grassy fields alongside it were still flattened, lying soddy and limp with small pools remaining in some areas. Eventually Tandon lost sight of the river as it made its way, unseen, to meet its bigger sister, the Buffalo River, known simply to the locals as the "Big Buffalo." He had all but forgotten what he had seen until he found the turnoff and spun the steering wheel in its direction.

He had only gone a few feet when several visions and sounds assaulted his senses. The first thing he noticed was that the Big Buffalo was flooded. Like the other, there were signs of it having receded some, but with the hundreds of springs and tributaries running into it it was still at a dangerous level.

At first, as he slowly crept to its bank, he noticed nothing but nature around him. Then, looking straight ahead along the road, he saw the back of the red car he had been searching for. Initially, Tandon was elated, having finally found JulieAnn, but that feeling was flushed away just as quickly as the debris in the river when he realized where she was.

Stopping only a few feet from the water's edge,

Tandon jumped out of the truck and ran into the water, noting its raging strength, and stopped before it could sweep him off his feet. Tandon looked closer and was relieved to see JulieAnn's silhouette in the driver's seat. He also noted the steam seeping out from under the hood of the car. Actually, as he surveyed the scene, he realized JulieAnn was in no real physical harm. She was on a low water bridge and the water came to less than half the height of the door, and granted, she was rocking some, but he would have bet money that she wasn't going anywhere. And though the engine had gotten wet he was sure that after a short wait it would probably start right up again.

Taking a deep breath Tandon yelled, "JulieAnn!" He could see her window was open, but it was evident she couldn't hear him. Cupping his hands around his mouth, he tried again. "JulieAnn!" This time he saw her stick her head out and look straight ahead to the other side of the river, then, when she didn't see anyone, turned to look back.

Tandon did not expect to see the depth of fear that he saw in her face. It threw him off and caused a surge of fear to swell in himself. He waved his arms about until she returned it, more frantic than he cared to see. She was clearly petrified.

Cupping his mouth again, he yelled, "Are you okay?" careful to say each word clearly.

She heard him. Nodding her head in large up and down movements she answered yelling back, "Yes!"

Tandon thought it was probably too soon, but

suggested loudly, "Try to start the car!" She nodded, then disappeared inside. He heard a couple of clicks, then nothing.

JulieAnn stuck her head back out. "What should I do?" she asked.

He had to think about that. "Wait!" he yelled.

"What?"

"Wait!"

She nodded in understanding and watched him, waiting for some instructions. The look in her eyes was killing him. He knew she'd been out there only a short time, but being alone and not sure if her car would be swept away or not… he could understand her fear. One thing was certain. He couldn't just leave her out there alone. It might be awhile and she'd only become more frightened. He had to get out there.

Turning, he ran back to the truck and looked in the back for rope. Bingo! He dragged the rope out. It was sturdy enough, but he still had a problem. It would be too dangerous to try and pull the car out with the truck. The rope wasn't thick enough for that anyway. Then, too, there was nothing on the car to attach the rope to.

What else could he do? He knew he couldn't just walk out there. He'd end up down river needing help of his own. Turning his head, he looked up the river trying to think. He saw a branch floating downstream and eyed it, his imagination working. As it neared the car a light in his head went on.

Running into the water, he yelled to JulieAnn, "I will be right there!"

"No!" she yelled, waving him back.

Tandon ignored her as he stripped off his shirt and threw it on the ground beyond the rivers reach. Then came his heavy work boots and socks. Grabbing the rope he ran up river along the soggy bank about as far as the rope would stretch allowing him to reach the car. Fortunately for him, it was the longest single piece of rope he'd ever seen. Finding a tree narrow enough, so as not to waste too much rope tying it around it, yet strong enough to hold his weight and the force of the water, he wrapped the rope around the trunk and quickly tied a knot. The other end he tied around his waist. "Okay," he breathed.

With a quick check of the slack, to make sure it wouldn't catch on anything, he stepped into the water. Trying to ignore its cold temperature, he waded out. He had only gone a couple of inches before the ground disappeared beneath him and he found himself falling full length into the pulsing water. Immediately swept up in the current, he gasped. Then instinct and determination took over. Using every ounce of strength just to stay afloat, he worked his powerful arms and legs steering himself to the center of the river, intent on putting himself in the direct path of the car. A couple of times his feet came in painful contact with rocks he couldn't see under the surface, but he ignored it, his concentration focused on only one thing. Before he knew it, he was almost on top of the car.

"Grab my hand!" JulieAnn yelled.

Just then he slammed into the driver's door. His feet wanted to go under but he kicked, grabbing with one hand at the door where the window had been rolled down, and with the other, JulieAnn's forearm. They clung that way for what seemed an eternity while Tandon caught his breath. "Okay, I'm ready," he finally breathed.

JulieAnn, still holding him tightly, carefully and quickly scooted her lower half back to the passenger side making room for Tandon. "Ready?" she asked. He could only nod. "Okay...Go!" she ordered and pulled on him with everything she had.

Tandon kicked and pulled as hard as he could, but the suction of the water was stronger. "I can't get my legs up!" he said, his voice straining. The next thing he knew, his head was being pushed down, then after feeling a weight momentarily press upon his back, felt his pants being tugged up uncomfortably at the back and he was being hauled into the car. While some of his length still hung out the window the majority of him was lying in JulieAnn's lap, panting.

"Are you alright?" she asked, looking down at him, catching her own breath.

"Yeah," he said on an exhale.

"What were you thinking?" she asked, sounding angry all of a sudden.

Tandon looked at her surprised, then grinned wearily. "Well, I always wanted to be a knight in shining armor," he said.

"Don't get fresh with me. You could have gotten killed!"

"Why JulieAnn, I didn't know you cared," he said, flashing her his best smile.

Furiously, she pushed him up and off of her, fairly folding him back in half until, with some awkward maneuvering, he was able to get his feet in and right himself behind the wheel.

"I'm not kidding!" she scolded, continuing where she'd left off. "That was a stupid thing to do!"

"Would you like me to leave?" he asked, playing coy. "As you can see I'm still attached to the rope. I suppose I could jump out and use whatever strength I have left to pull myself back until I'm safely on land. Or, I could take my chances, cut the rope off and float downstream...I just hope I don't drown from exhaustion," he finished, adding a heavy sigh for effect. Before he had finished, JulieAnn had turned her face away from him and he could tell from her sunken cheeks that she was biting them, determined to keep from laughing.

"Well, frankly, I'm a bit tired. I think I'll have to pick door number two. Wish me luck." The last he said with mock bravery. Tandon had crawled out to sit in the open window and was about to draw out a leg when JulieAnn stopped him with a reluctant laugh. Tandon tilted his head down to get a peek at her. Boy, he'd missed her laugh.

"Knock it off," she said trying to hide her humor. "Get back in here."

"If you insist."

"I insist," she said, letting loose a little giggle.

Settled in behind the wheel once again, Tandon stole a glance at JulieAnn. As soon as she started to face him, though, he whipped his back, looking straight ahead, self-conscious. After another moment had passed, he couldn't help it, he stole another look, and this time, caught her head snapping back. Reflexively, his did the same.

Feeling strangely squirmy, and reluctant to steal another peak, Tandon drummed his fingers on the dashboard. Minutes ticked by with only the rhythm of his rolling digits to keep time. Then, without thinking, he blurted, "Do you have any cards?"

CHAPTER SEVENTEEN

The car swayed gently from side to side rocking its inhabitants as if it was a cradle; the sound of the water lapping against its side soothing Tandon and JulieAnn into silence. Their shared laughter, only moments earlier, had been a welcome release from the pent up tension each had felt and for that brief time they were happy. But that feeling soon faded with the laughter and in its place, quietude.

After a time Tandon sensed a certain tension growing in the air and he became uncomfortable. He knew this was an awkward situation for JulieAnn, for both of them, but it would only grow more unbearable, trapped as they were for the time being, if they didn't speak.

The thought made him remember the car, the reason he was sitting there, soaked, in the first place. Raising his hand to the keys dangling from the ignition, Tandon said, "Guess we should see if it'll start." Then he turned the key. There was a moment when the engine turned over, but just as quickly it died. "Better," he said, "but it'll still be awhile."

Tandon watched JulieAnn roll down her window and saw the concern in her profile as she looked at the water rushing down the river. "It's okay. We're not going anywhere," he consoled. "As soon as the engine dries we can back out of here and be on our way."

At his words JulieAnn looked at him, her expression unreadable.

Returning her look, Tandon wondered if now was a good time to talk to her. He had a lot he wanted to say - it was why he had chased her down after all, but he could see she was still nervous. Would now really be an appropriate time?

While he was debating, JulieAnn spoke. "I'm sorry," she whispered.

Tandon saw her sincerity, but drew a blank as to her meaning. "Sorry for what?" he asked, curious.

JulieAnn expelled a delicate sigh. "Jess," she answered, then looked out the front window. "He should never have gone to see you."

Tandon was not surprised to find her thoughts, her subject matter, running along the same line with his. That JulieAnn, herself, would lead them into it, however, after having run off to avoid it, and him, was surprising. Beyond that, though, he was touched by the depth of feeling he heard in her tone and saw in her profile. And despite knowing there could be more than one meaning to her words, he chose to follow his instinct, the instant warmth that permeated throughout his being, and said softly, "I'm glad he did."

Immediately she turned, her mouth open slightly, her eyes wide and passionate. "How can you say that? I mean, after how we treated you? How I treated you?" JulieAnn looked down at her lap, "Why would you even want to come back?"

Tandon smiled slightly, "Your brother's very convincing." JulieAnn flinched at that and he was sorry. He realized that, to JulieAnn's ears, it sounded as if he'd said, "I didn't want to come, but Jess persuaded me to." So he amended it by saying, "There is nothing Jess could have said to make me come if I didn't want to. I am here because I want to be here," he said firmly.

JulieAnn looked deep into his eyes as if searching for confirmation. Tandon was unable to tell whether she found what she was looking for as she turned away. "I'm afraid you've wasted your trip," she said. "Nothing's changed. Jess should have known better." The last she added almost angrily.

"If by, 'nothing's changed,' you mean your concern for your family, then you needn't worry." JulieAnn's head snapped back in surprise. "They've had a change of heart," he said.

"But...that day..." JulieAnn was frowning, confused.

Tandon put a hand up to stop her. "That was a bad day, I know, and we all got a little carried away," Tandon paused, thinking, needing her to understand. He turned his body to face her, hiking his leg up to rest it on his seat. "What I mean is this has nothing to do with the issues surrounding the river. Their concern for it is still the same."

JulieAnn's frown deepened as she sought to understand his meaning.

"This has to do with you," he explained. "According to Jess, they've seen the sacrifice you've made for them," at that, JulieAnn's face turned crimson, "and to make a long story short, they want you to be happy."

For a moment she said nothing, then realizing the implication of his words said, "They have all been discussing this? Me?"

"Apparently so," he said and watched her face. JulieAnn was clearly mortified. The idea that her family had gotten together to discuss her personal life was obviously troubling to her.

Tandon witnessed the changing of her churning thoughts with every twisting expression that passed across her face until finally settling on the last of Tandon's comments.

With her mouth forming a perfect 'O', JulieAnn became, what was for her, unusually uppity. "Who are they to say I'm not happy. Of course I'm happy. I'm always happy!" JulieAnn huffed making it a struggle for Tandon to hold back the sudden grin that wanted to erupt at her childish response. "All this time I thought I was doing them a favor. Now they think they're going to do me a favor!" Then she slapped her leg as a new thought came to her and turned to him, mirroring his posture, as though he were an equally innocent and tormented soul. "I'll bet no one even considered that we might have moved on. For all they know we're seeing other people, and here they are trying to interfere."

At her comment, Tandon's hope and confidence dissolved. The uncertainty was back and he had to know, from the only one who could answer him, if the man he saw at her house was, in fact, a part of her life or if anyone else was for that matter.

Interrupting JulieAnn, who was clearly steeped in outraged thoughts, he said, "JulieAnn?" Gaining her attention he looked directly into her eyes. "Have you? Moved on? Are you seeing other people?"

"Well, yes!" she said automatically, distracted. "I mean…No!" she corrected, frowning. Looking at Tandon and seeing his face, JulieAnn realized, with sudden clarity, what she had been saying. "Oh, Tandon. I'm so sorry," she said, her expression crestfallen, her eyes closing in dismay.

In the intense silence that followed both looked away from the other and out of their own windows, neither satisfied with the way the conversation was going. Tandon didn't know what to make of her answer. He wasn't even certain he had gotten an answer.

Then, without warning, and obviously unable to hold it back any longer, JulieAnn blurted out, "Are you seeing anyone?"

They turned to one another.

"No," Tandon said, then admitted, "I haven't since I left here."

"Oh," was all JulieAnn said.

It occurred to Tandon that he might not necessarily want JulieAnn thinking he hadn't wanted to or that he'd spent all of his time pining away over her, so he added, "I didn't have time, what with my schedule and all." It was, after all, the truth.

"I see," she said. "How is your job, aside from keeping you busy, I mean?" she asked as though they were only having a polite conversation.

"It was all right," he answered.

Immediately, JulieAnn picked up on his reference. "Was?" she queried.

Tandon studied JulieAnn wondering how much detail he should go into, if any. With a deep breath he explained in short, "I quit my job."

* * *

"No! Oh, Tandon, you didn't!" Tandon's unexpected announcement came as a crushing blow to JulieAnn, as if she had just experienced a personal loss of her own. "But why?" she asked when he didn't immediately respond. "You loved that job. It's all you ever wanted to do."

Tandon tried to shrug it off as if it was of no real consequence. "I guess I needed a change of scenery," he said nonchalantly.

JulieAnn could only stare at him. Somehow that didn't sound right. There had to be more to it than that, she was sure. Different ideas formed as she attempted to probe into his meaning. Had he gotten tired of his job? It was possible, but she didn't think so. Perhaps he had gotten fired, or demoted, and he didn't want to admit it for fear of embarrassment or shame. Again, no. Too unlikely.

JulieAnn was stretching her imagination as far as she could, running the gamut from everything minute to borderline extreme, without success when a shocking thought came to her. She looked at Tandon afraid to ask, though much more fearful of the answer. "Is it because of Jess? Did he say something to convince you to quit?" She held her breath for the answer.

Tandon seemed to study her for a moment before responding, "Jess had nothing to do with it. I had quit before he showed up."

JulieAnn expelled her breath, grateful for that bit of news. But she still wasn't satisfied. "Then why, Tandon? Why would you quit?" She waited expectantly for his answer. She felt it was an important one...a serious one. It had to be. He had put too much of himself into it to just pull away from it over some flimsy excuse.

After a moment he sighed and answered, "I just didn't see things the way I once had."

JulieAnn had instinctively begun to open her mouth, to ask him what things he was talking about, but stopped short of doing so when he looked away. There was something queer about the way he did it that warned her not to pursue the matter any further so she closed her mouth reluctantly. Staring at the back of his head she realized, that for whatever reason, Tandon was evading her question. And it hurt. It hurt to know that he didn't feel that he could confide in her. But so be it. If he didn't want to talk about it, she decided, she wouldn't push him.

A soothing breeze blew in through the windows drawing JulieAnn's attention to the river. She watched as the water slapped against a tree that had, at one time, fallen to lie horizontal to the direct flow that now beat upon it. She saw the backlog of debris hovering about boulders that protruded out from the murky dirt and sand soiled water as it became trapped by the swirling, cyclonic movement. Without realizing it, JulieAnn had begun to relax. It seemed the river was working its own magic over her, bringing her to a heightened level of awareness, awakening her senses while at the same time creating a hypnotic effect.

As her lids slowly lowered and her head leaned back against the headrest, she became acutely aware of the sharp earthy smells carried in on the breeze. The water held a slight odor of fish and the mold that was beginning to grow along the overly watered banks. She even caught a waft of something sweet smelling that she assumed were wild flowers hiding nearby. It brought an appreciative smile to her face. She was also aware of the sounds. The soft rustling of the leaves; bull frogs croaking as they sunned themselves on the rocks; birds carrying on in the tree tops and fluttering about on the ground.

It was all so perfect, so wonderful. JulieAnn sighed contentedly, then gasped...her eyes flying open to stare, unseen, at the visor. The river! Of course! That's what Tandon had meant. That's what he saw differently. It was the Park Service. He didn't agree with them anymore. He didn't believe in their cause to own the river. He was on their side.

She wondered why it hadn't occurred to her before. She wanted to giggle. Now she could understand why he hadn't wanted to tell her. Men's pride. To think he couldn't admit he had changed his mind. JulieAnn shook her head slightly as the corners of her mouth lifted. He was one of them now.

* * *

Tandon wasn't sure why JulieAnn was looking at him the way she was but he certainly wasn't going to complain. It was good to see her smile. Just the warmth he felt from it was enough to remove the chill from beneath his wet clothes.

As he returned her smile, Tandon felt the mood between them shifting, moving to a higher level, a better place. It brought him back to happier days. Days when it was only the two of them in the world. Where the sun always shone on them, a halo of love and devotion, tenderness and simplicity. Where the earth pulsed, alive with vibrant color and tranquil sounds, and where the breath of life itself was intoxicating. A perfect bouquet arranged just for them. He wanted that back.

"JulieAnn," Tandon said, "there's something I need to tell you."

JulieAnn shifted her body, facing him again. Her expression was attentive. "Okay. I'm listening," she said.

Again, Tandon was mesmerized by her eyes, their intensity as she looked at him, waiting for him to go on. He nearly lost his train of thought but forced himself to focus. He cleared his throat. "JulieAnn," he began, "we've known each other a long time, and I know that I've done things to hurt you,"

"No, Tandon, don't."

"Please. I have to say this."

JulieAnn's look grew thoughtful as she yielded to Tandon's plea.

"I botched things up between you and I. We had a good thing going once, but I put myself first. I had an idea of what I wanted for my life and I went for it, without ever considering what you wanted."

Although JulieAnn was shaking her head, her downcast eyes revealed the painful truth in what he said.

"I've said it before and I'll say it again, I was a stupid kid. I was selfish and bull headed. I was determined to have things my own way. Not you or my father, or even my dying mother could have had an impact on me. And I pray to God that none of you blame yourselves, because it was all me. Last year…"

"Last year I messed everything up," JulieAnn said earnestly.

"No, you didn't," Tandon said, shaking his head. "You did the right thing. You did what I had never done, which is look out for the people who love you." Tandon smiled tenderly, "I wouldn't have expected anything less from you. That's what I like about you. You're kind and generous. You're unselfish to the point of neglecting yourself and…"

JulieAnn chuckled self-consciously, "I think you have me confused with someone else," she said, tucking her chin into her chest. "You're making me sound perfect, and I'm not."

To Tandon, she was - except for one thing.

"You're only fault," he said softly, "is loving me." He heard JulieAnn's breath catch in her throat as she raised her eyes to his. He saw they were wet with tears and it tugged at his heart. "I've always known you loved me. I could see it when you looked at me. When you talked to me, I could hear it in your voice." Tandon smiled, remembering, "Your whole being lit up when you were with me. You were an open book that way," he said.

JulieAnn's tears were running down her cheeks now. She tried to swallow.

"The one thing you didn't know, what I didn't let you see, was that I love you too." He heard a whimper escape from her throat. "I still love you," he said hoarsely, surprising himself when he felt tears spring to his eyes. Tandon swallowed hard, suppressing them. "Last year I asked you to give us a try, and I know," he added, rushing on when he saw her mouth open to explain, "that you had obligations to your family. I understand. I do. But circumstances have changed, and…I hope…" Tandon never got to finish his comment. JulieAnn moved so quickly that he hadn't had time to react. Not that he would have. That is, other than to return her kiss.

At first, when her lips had met his, it was with a sudden force, pushing him backwards against the door, shocking him into submission. It seemed that all of her weight was leaning into it, holding him captive. It was not a bad thing. Then, after a moment, she began to loosen her hold, until for just a moment, they were separated.

With his eyes closed, he could feel her warm breath fanning his mouth. He could taste a trace of saltiness on his lips, left behind from her tears. He couldn't wait any longer. Of its own volition,

Tandon's head began its descent, his movements, so tormentingly slow, were barely perceptive. Despite the almost nonexistent distance that separated them, it seemed as though a lifetime were passing by as he craned his neck, drawing himself closer - aiming instinctively for the object of his desire.

When their lips finally met, softly touching, a shock ran through Tandon, rendering him helpless and still, immovable while the rest of the world vanished from existence. He forgot about the present, the good and the bad, even their history together with both its love and pain. As they kissed, their experience became a new one - a union no longer born of a boy and a girl, but of a man and a woman. Their feelings no longer those of their younger selves where lust and emotional admissions of love were controlled by raging hormones, but by something far greater and deeper than anything they had ever experienced.

After a time they pulled apart, breaking the kiss, but not the intimacy. Tandon's gaze roamed over JulieAnn taking in her smoldering eyes and working his way across her perfectly shaped features before finally resting on her swollen lips.

He was studying them, when she spoke. "Tandon," she said beseechingly. He looked into her beautiful eyes. "Tell me again. What you said earlier."

Tandon knew what she wanted to hear, and he was only too willing to accommodate her. "JulieAnn, I love you," he said, enjoying the sound of it as it rolled off of his tongue. He said it again. "I love you." Then again, over and over, adding speed each time, "I love you. I love you, I love you..." JulieAnn was laughing as tears rolled down her face. Tandon stopped then, suddenly, and looked deep into her eyes. In a very serious voice, thick with emotion, he said one last time, "I love you."

JulieAnn, too, had become very still, as she realized the full implication of his words. Then, with a single tear rolling down her cheek, she whispered back, "I love you." The silence that followed, as they looked at one another, was not a strained one. There was no tension or awkwardness...no agitation. There was only two people whose lives had once again been brought together. Only now they knew there was nothing to separate them.

Just then, they heard a raucous blare of a horn and regrettably tore their gazes apart to see a car parked on the other side of the river with a man standing beside it waving to them.

Tandon stuck his head out of the window as the man stepped closer and yelled, "Do you need any help?"

Tandon looked in at JulieAnn for a moment, their love pouring out between them, then faced the man. Cupping his hands, he yelled, "No. We are okay," and shook his head for emphasis.

"Are you sure?"

"Yes. We're fine," he nodded in large rocking motions.

The man lifted his arms out at his sides helplessly, then turned and left.

Tandon slid back into his seat facing JulieAnn.

"We don't need any help?" she asked, with humor sneaking into her gaze.

Tandon smiled at JulieAnn with adoring affection. "Not anymore," he said, then raised his hand to the ignition and turned the key. It started right up.

He turned to her then, pulling her to him - their faces only a breath apart and repeated, "Not anymore

CHAPTER EIGHTEEN

Over the next four days, Tandon and JulieAnn spent every waking moment together, making sure to utilize as much time as was possible in a twenty-four hour period, unwilling as they were to waste any precious moments apart.

The routine was the same every day. Each morning, not long after dawn, using a spare truck loaned to him by Jess, Tandon would show up at JulieAnn's door with flowers and a ready kiss that would make her toes curl. Then, together, they were off.

Every day's destination was a new one. Their first day out they drove to Eureka Springs and toured the historical town on foot. While JulieAnn admired the unique designs and perfect contrasting of colors on the old Victorian homes, "They're like large doll houses," Tandon, in turn admired the fine masonry work of the old buildings lining the main business center that were built between the late

1800's and early 1900's, "You can tell people poured their heart and soul into these buildings. You don't see that kind of quality craftsmanship, these days." Their favorite part of the day, however, was when they took a ride on a white horse drawn carriage to visit the town's most famous hotel, The Crescent Hotel. "It's said to be haunted," their driver warned over his shoulder.

After marveling over its outer limestone facing and its truly expansive size, they entered into its magnificent entrance where they were immediately taken with the massive fireplace. Guided by the hotel's manager they visited a variety of socializing rooms, the top floor balconies with their spectacular views and even the basement, where it is believed to have once been a morgue. With each turn, it seemed, something horrible and mysterious had once happened and the ghosts of the unfortunate were said to roam.

"It is kind of eerie," JulieAnn whispered.

They were definitely in agreement on that.

Their second day was spent mostly in the car as they made the hour and a half trip up to Springfield, Missouri. For a while they walked through a large mall, mostly window shopping but occasionally entering if there was something that caught their attention. They drove through the city with JulieAnn oohing and aahing over its size and the amount of stores and restaurants, and well, just about everything since her small hometown was extremely lacking in comparison. "It would take a lifetime for Jasper to get this full!" she said. Then they stopped at, what was to JulieAnn, the largest ice cream shop she had ever seen. And was it busy! They finally had their turn at the counter where they both ordered waffle cones to overflowing.

Tandon requested his ice cream be black cherry. He licked his lips, "Mmm, my favorite," he said.

JulieAnn scrunched up her nose, then requested her own favorites. A sweet concoction of butter pecan and mint chocolate chip, and that topped by a colorful scoop of rainbow sherbet. Clearly pleased with her decision she turned to Tandon and saw that his face had become so pinched that she could barely see his eyeballs. "What!"

"Are you going to eat that?"

She smiled wide, "Just watch me."

In the space of one minute they had paid for and were handed their cones by a pimply faced kid who tried, not too successfully, to hide his own disgust at her choices.

JulieAnn couldn't help herself. "What!" she said for the second time.

Tandon, not missing the exchange, burst into laughter, causing more than a few pretty females to turn their heads.

On their third day together Tandon and JulieAnn journeyed again to Missouri, but this time visiting Branson. Since neither of them had ever been to a live show they decided it would be fun to see, what was said to be, "Branson's first show" - The Baldknobbers. And what a great decision that had been. With the entertainers encouraging the audience's participation, the two clapped their hands, stomped their feet and sang along to the country, gospel, and patriotic songs along with the rest of the audience. It was all so terrific, but their favorite parts were the comedy skits. Their outlandish costumes and hilarious exaggerations of back-o'-the-woods country folk had both laughing so hard their sides hurt. JulieAnn even had tears running down her face. Later, they went out to eat at a mom and pop restaurant and ordered juicy burgers with all of the fixings they could top them with and homemade apple pie's a la mode for dessert.

The time JulieAnn and Tandon spent together was a surreal experience. Even when they were visually distracted, or otherwise, there seemed to always be a light, airy feeling about them, as if they were floating - a sort of out-of-body experience. It was a heady sensation. But they were in love. Anyone with two eyes could see that. No matter what they were doing, they were always together, literally, in physical contact. Whether they were driving or walking, eating, or just sitting and relaxing, they had to be close and touching.

And it was in the same manner that they found themselves the following day, snuggling together aboard their rented pontoon on Bull Shoals Lake, when JulieAnn broached the subject of Tandon's father. "You know," she began, careful to keep her tone carefree, "I bet your father would love to know you're back."

She was leaning against Tandon with her back to his chest, his arms folded around her, when she felt him stiffen and hold his breath. Then, just as quickly, he recovered, giving her a squeeze. "Let's not talk about it right now," he said. "Let's just enjoy the moment."

JulieAnn was content with that. Besides, she knew there'd be another opportunity to bring it up. "All right," she said.

Tandon knew better. He sighed and tried to sit up, urging JulieAnn to also. "Okay," he said, conceding, "I know you're never going to let this go, so let's just get it over with."

JulieAnn smiled, "How about tomorrow?"

"How about tomorrow what?"

"How about tomorrow we go see your dad?"

"We?" Tandon said, raising his brows.

"Yeah, sure. Why not?"

Tandon's chuckle was not a humorous one. "Well, for one thing, he doesn't consider me family anymore. I'm dead to him."

"You know that's not true. He's just being stubborn."

Tandon refrained from comment.

"You quit your job. I'd bet he'd be glad to hear that," she said earnestly.

Tandon snorted, "I bet he would." Then, "We'll probably just end up fighting. I wouldn't want you to see that."

"I won't," she smiled. "Gentlemen are always on their best behavior in front of a lady."

"Boy, are you sheltered," he chortled.

"If they're not, then they're not a gentleman. And I'm quite certain that you, my love, are a gentleman." With that, JulieAnn wrapped her arms tightly around Tandon and tipped her face up to him charmingly.

Tandon looked down at JulieAnn. Boy was it

going to be hard resisting her. Not that he'd ever want to.

"Tandon, give him another chance. Who knows? He may surprise you."

He let out a long breath through his nostrils. "You drive a hard bargain lady, you know that?" She just smiled and waited expectantly. Tandon's gaze moved to the horizon. "Oh, all right. If it'll make you happy." JulieAnn giggled, juggling his waistline. "But if this doesn't work out, you have to promise not to bring it up again," he said seriously.

"It's a promise," she said, then promptly kissed him. "So," she said, "tomorrow morning you'll come over and I'll make you breakfast," she kissed him again, "and afterwards we'll go see your father."

Tandon laughed. "If you can cook as well as you manipulate, then I'm in big trouble."

"Awe, do I worry you, Mr. Bowman?"

Tandon chuckled, "Most definitely, Ms. Peterson."

* * *

It was shortly after eleven the following morning when Tandon and JulieAnn arrived at the home of Isaac Bowman. Outwardly Tandon was a model of composure and confidence, but inwardly he was a jumble of nerves. And why wouldn't he be? Their last visits had been terrible. So, who could blame him for not being eager to go through it again. Oh, how he hated this. *If I could just be anywhere else but here*, he thought.

They remained in JulieAnn's car, with the engine off, looking around the yard. "Maybe we missed him," Tandon said. "He may have gone to town or is visiting someone. We might have to come back some other time."

JulieAnn only smiled and put her hand on his thigh, understanding his hesitancy.

Tandon pointed then, "Look, his truck is gone," he said like a zealous child.

JulieAnn suppressed a giggle. "It is, but I'm just going to knock on the door and make sure." She scrambled out of the passenger seat before he could stop her and bounded up to the porch and knocked.

Tandon reached her a moment later looking very thankful that it hadn't yet been answered. "See? He's not here," he said.

JulieAnn had to concede that he was right, but as they made their way down the steps, they both heard a sound to their right and turned in that direction.

"Do you hear that?" JulieAnn asked.

Tandon closed his eyes, grimacing, "I want to say no."

At that moment they saw a tractor come into view with a familiar figure sitting atop it.

"It's your dad."

"He's baling hay," Tandon said then brightened. "Well, we should go anyhow. He'll be doing this for hours and…"

"He's not that far away. Let's go out there and talk to him."

"No, that's not a good idea. He never liked being interrupted." Tandon had learned that first hand as a child.

JulieAnn turned to Tandon looking very serious

and took both his hands in hers. "Tandon," she said, "putting this off is only going to make it harder in the long run."

He sighed, knowing she was right.

"What do you say we take the risk and just go out there and get it over with?"

Tandon looked back to the field and to the man who, only last year, he had faced similarly and failed. Would another attempt make any difference? Somehow he doubted it, but for JulieAnn, he would try. "All right," he said, and together, with hands locked, they headed into the field.

* * *

Tandon and JulieAnn made their way to the center of the field crunching over the cut stems and leaves of a variety of grasses that now made up the hay that lay dried and raked in long rows along the ground awaiting their turn for baling. Neither said much as they walked, but both noticed when Isaac spotted them. Often Isaac's head turned to look behind him to gauge the baler's progress, and it was during one of those checks that they saw his head stop in mid turn to focus on them before continuing with his work.

Tandon wasn't sure if his father had recognized him or not, but the possibility that he had and did not stop made him very nervous and his grip on JulieAnn's hand tightened. JulieAnn placed her free hand over their clasped ones and lightly loosened his fingers.

Tandon realized what she was doing and apologized. "Sorry," he said with feeling.

She smiled, "It's okay." Then she encouraged,

"Try to stay calm. Let it happen on its own."

"Letting it happen at all is what I'm worried about," he said.

It was JulieAnn's turn to squeeze Tandon's hand. "Have faith," she said and smiled reassuringly at him.

That's easy for you to say, he thought, but didn't say so.

Isaac Bowman made a pass over another windrow before he stopped the tractor, shut off the engine, and climbed down. By this time Tandon and JulieAnn had gained enough ground that they could easily see Isaac's features and so Tandon assumed that, likewise, his father had also seen and recognized him and was merely waiting to chew him out.

Minutes later, with JulieAnn urging him along, the two reached the tractor and Isaac, who was wiping beads of perspiration from his face and neck with his handkerchief. Tandon stopped a safe distance of five to six feet from his father, but was surprised when JulieAnn let go of his hand and finished the distance to give Isaac a hug and kiss on the cheek, though that was not even as shocking as it was seeing his father returning her affection with his own…and a smile to boot. Tandon couldn't even remember the last time he had seen his father smile. It had to have been some time before he had moved away at age seventeen.

"Mr. Bowman, how are you?" JulieAnn inquired gaily, taking a step back.

"Pretty busy lately," Isaac answered in his gruff way.

"Looks like another good year for haying."

Isaac nodded, "It got a little iffy with all the rain, but I'm managing." Tandon noticed his father kept his eyes averted. Isaac hadn't looked at him once.

"How's your new housekeeper coming along?" JulieAnn asked keeping the conversation light.

Isaac huffed, "Estelle? She's more of a pest than anything. Keeps trying to get me to 'do my share'. I have to keep reminding that woman that that's what I pay her for."

Tandon couldn't understand why JulieAnn thought that that was so funny. To him, it sounded like his father was the same pain in the arse he'd always been. And he had never found it funny in the least. As for the new cleaning lady, he hadn't even thought to ask JulieAnn about that. He was glad to know she wasn't taking care of it anymore, though.

Tandon was growing increasingly perturbed at his father's obvious attempt to ignore him. After all, what did his father think…that he was standing out there for his health? Well go ahead, he thought, play your childish game, but don't expect me to help you.

Out of spite, more than anything else, Tandon forced his presence on his father. "Hi dad," he said. His tone was flat, but with a trace of animosity. It worked. His father finally turned to him, acknowledging him, though it may have only been due to JulieAnn's presence as she stood by smiling.

"Tandon," Isaac said, mimicking his son's tone.

In the tense silence that followed, Tandon could see, from the corner of his eye, JulieAnn's head swiveling from side to side as she looked from one to the other. Then she walked over to Tandon and stood beside him taking his hand in hers. She smiled excitedly at Isaac. "Isn't it wonderful, Mr. Bowman? Tandon's back."

Isaac's gaze had fastened on their joined hands. "Yes," he drawled, "I can see that." He looked at Tandon again, "I suppose I should ask why?"

JulieAnn looked up at Tandon and gave his hand a conspicuous squeeze, urging him to say something. When he didn't immediately respond, she encouraged, "Go on Tandon, tell him why."

Tandon knew that once he said it he'd quickly regret it. And he was right. "I quit my job," he said.

There was a pause as his father let that sink in, then true to character, Isaac threw back his head and laughed and continued to as he spit out, "That's fantastic! Not only do you quit on your family and friends, but now, you quit on your job. *The* job! Your dream job!"

Tandon looked at JulieAnn and saw that her smile had disappeared. That touched a nerve in him. His father's attitude was not surprising. Hell, it was typical. But to act like that in front of JulieAnn...it was uncalled for.

Before he could think of a suitable reply, his father raised his arms and bellowed, "Ladies and gentlemen! Meet Tandon...the prodigal son! He went off to live the good life, but couldn't handle it. And now he returns for forgiveness!"

JulieAnn looked crushed. Tandon wanted to punch his father. "How dare you," Tandon growled between his teeth.

"How dare I? How…dare…*I*?"

Tandon could see his father was losing control and wanting to fight. He was definitely not going to subject JulieAnn to that. He turned to her then, "I'm sorry, I tried. Let's just go."

JulieAnn didn't argue as they turned away. After a time she said, "Tandon, I'm sorry. I didn't realize. I should have never asked you to…"

Tandon put his arm around her, "It's okay. It's not your fault."

They had almost reached the edge of the field when they heard Isaac yell. "Why did you quit?"

JulieAnn slowed her steps and turned.

"No, JulieAnn. Just ignore him," Tandon said and tried to steer her along with him, but she stopped, planting her feet firmly to the spot.

"Maybe I can fix this," she said, her voice hopeful.

"You can't," he said. "There's no point."

"I have to try," she said and gently, but firmly, removed her arm from his grasp and headed back to Isaac.

Tandon stood there watching her, debating whether or not to follow her. Then, almost immediately, he concluded, "Idiot. Of course you have to. You can't just leave her out there alone at his mercy." So he began to follow her back, hoping his father wouldn't do more harm before he could get there.

JulieAnn hadn't been alone with Isaac for very long when Tandon finally reached them. The first thing he noticed was that the mood seemed different and it made him feel uneasy. They were both facing him, JulieAnn smiling and Isaac looking at him, but there was something very different about it.

Tandon stood in the same place as he had earlier, and again JulieAnn came to stand at his side. He looked at her closely, wondering what had been said that had her beaming at him that way. Then he looked at his father. The change was unmistakable. It made him nervous again.

No one had said anything, then Isaac cleared his throat. "I…I'm sorry for my behavior before," he said awkwardly.

Tandon's jaw dropped. Had he just heard right?

Before Tandon could recover, Isaac was clearing his throat again. It sounded as if he had something large and monstrous lodged there. "I want you to know that…you've earned a second chance. If you want it," Isaac said.

This time Tandon's brows rose. Have I indeed, he thought. What was going on here? He turned his head sharply to JulieAnn. "What did you say?"

"I simply explained why you quit," she said smiling, clearly very pleased with the outcome.

He frowned slightly. "And what was that, exactly."

"Oh, you know," she said and looped her arm through his, giving him a little snuggle. "Well," she said, "what do you think?"

What do I think? I think my nightmares have come back. But, of course, he didn't say that. Instead he just looked from one to the other, unsure of what to say. Though he should have. After all, he had asked for this very chance last year, but now that the opportunity was staring him in the face, he found it somehow...well, he wasn't quite sure.

Tandon and his father had grown so far apart and had remained that way for so long that it had become a kind of normalcy. And even of late, when this need had surfaced, Tandon had known that there was never really going to be a chance for them. Perhaps that was why he had made the attempt. Because he had felt safe. He had known it would never happen. But now that his father had changed all of that and made the offer, he didn't know what to do.

Questions skipped through his mind. Should he accept or shouldn't he? What would be expected of him? What did he expect of his father? Would they be able to return to the way things used to be? And when would that happen? Now... right away? Later? How long would it last? Only until their next fight? For some reason, Tandon was having a very hard time deciding what to do. Even when he told himself to follow his instinct, that that would be the right choice, he couldn't figure out what that was.

Then, unexpectedly, while he was looking at JulieAnn, he saw his mother's face and heard her words, urging him on her death bed to forget the problems between them. She was right, of course, and her advice had never been wrong. It may not have worked then, but maybe it could now. Tandon knew what he had to do.

With the woman he loved standing beside him, he faced his father. "I'll take it," he said, accepting his father's offer of a second chance.

Father and son looked at one another for a silent moment, then Isaac, slowly, held his hand out to Tandon. With a smile, and tears in her eyes, JulieAnn let go of Tandon's arm and stepped back, watching as his hand moved out. There was a split second hesitation, but he followed through, finally clasping his father's hand.

It was an unexpectedly emotional moment for Tandon as his father held his hand. He could feel a slight quiver and it touched him, though his father's face didn't reveal much. Isaac's voice cracked though when he said, "Welcome home."

Tandon couldn't help the tears that sprang to his eyes and made no effort to wipe them as they spilled down his cheeks. After a moment more, they released their grips and merely stood there.

JulieAnn finally came to their aid and asked Isaac, "Do you still keep some lemonade in the house?"

"Haven't had it in a while, but it should be there," Isaac answered, his voice still hoarse.

"Well, how about we head back to the house and I'll make us some," she offered.

Isaac remembered the baling and turned his head, "I need to finish this up, but you two go ahead."

"I'll help you with it tomorrow, if you like," Tandon said.

The silence that came after that was powerful as Isaac looked at his son. It might have been his imagination, but Tandon thought he saw a tear in his father's eye. Isaac turned away, though, before he could get a good look, and by the time he faced them again he was composed.

"I'll take it," Isaac said using his son's words.

And together they walked back to the house with Tandon flanked by two people that, only days ago, wanted nothing to do with him.

Wow.

It was all he could think.

CHAPTER NINETEEN

For Tandon, his first week back could only have been described as extraordinary. But when combined with the month that followed, it became something altogether indefinable. With a script seemingly written, produced and directed by a higher power, the world around Tandon took on a life of its own with himself and everyone connected to him as fortunate participants of an act gone right. And it was spectacular. A box office hit. To Tandon, life could not have gotten any better.

His relationship with JulieAnn, which had only just been rekindled, grew at an astounding rate as they continued seeing one another daily, allowing for no interference other than JulieAnn's return to work after her brief respite to be with Tandon, and the evenings, when finally tired and needing rest they parted company.

Though they were together, sometimes late into those evenings, and though their feelings had grown quite intense for one another, they never allowed themselves permission to venture into that place of no return. Tandon knew the beliefs JulieAnn had grown up with. They were the same his mother and the church had instilled in him, though he, admittedly, had strayed from those teachings from time to time. And whether JulieAnn had stuck to her beliefs or not was irrelevant because their relationship was different. It was one-of-a-kind, unique, and Tandon wanted it to be treated as such and not defile it in any way. It was something they both agreed to, though neither had spoken of it out loud for the words themselves were unnecessary.

It was at those moments of greatest temptation when, with great difficulty and regret, they separated themselves and each returned to their own haven, that they would lie down and close their eyes and dream of that day when they would finally be together. It was a day that, Tandon knew, was fast approaching.

In the sunlit hours when they were forced to be apart, Tandon had worked to bridge the gap in his relationship with his father. And literally, he worked. An effort which, Tandon would come to believe, was the band aid that would cure their emotional friction. As promised, Tandon had helped his father with the baling of the hay - something he had balked at as a teenager, but which he now realized was not all that bad. Still, he wouldn't want to do it every day. When that job had been completed, they moved to tackle other projects: repairing the leaking roof, broken floor boards, and rusty faucets. Even painting the outside of the house a fresh coat of white.

It was an oddity, the two of them working alongside one another, but they did it, and without biting words of criticism and sarcasm. Instead, they kept to safe conversations and enjoyed each other's company, often joking and laughing in real joy.

There were a couple of moments while they worked that Tandon had looked at his father and felt a deep sadness over the wasted years - the enmity between them, but then he would catch himself and smile, grateful for the moment. He knew that this is what his mother would have wanted. He could almost see her smiling at them, nodding the way she sometimes did when she was pleased, and he knew that he had made the right decisions this time, with Jess' help of course.

It wasn't until early into his second week that Tandon would see Jess again. It was with a hint of déjà vu that Tandon answered the knock on his hotel room door to find Jess standing there. But, this time, Jess was all smiles.

Tandon spent an hour answering Jess' questions about what he and JulieAnn had done the previous week and telling him how grateful he was to Jess for having come to him despite the risk of hurting his sister. "Awe, I knew it would work out," Jess had laughed. Then Tandon happily answered yes to whether he thought he'd be sticking around or not. It was one of those decisions that didn't require much contemplation. It was a given, something he'd probably decided on while trapped on the river with JulieAnn. To do anything else was unconscionable.

"I'd like to buy a house, but I'll have to get something temporary," he told Jess, "an apartment or something until I can bring the rest of my things down. I'll have to move fast though. My rent's only paid up until the end of October. I'd hate to have to pay another whole month's rent if I don't have to."

That's when Jess made his second convincing proposal in weeks and offered Tandon a room at his place. "It's a small house and there are a lot of car parts lying around, but if you can handle that, there's a spare room you can use."

Tandon argued only once saying he didn't want to impose.

"First of all, I wouldn't be asking if it was going to be an imposition." Tandon had grinned at Jess' attempted sternness. "And I'm sure you made a lot more dough than myself, but staying in this hotel day after day can't be cheap."

And so, Tandon had accepted, grateful to get out of the small hotel room and also happy not to have to drive back and forth from Harrison to Jasper all of the time. And Jess was right, the hotel wasn't cheap. Money was getting tight what with the hotel quickly draining him and knowing he'd still owe on utilities in his apartment at the same time. He did intend to pay Jess though. He was no mooch.

"How can I pay you?" he asked.

Jess put his hand up, "Hey, let's just call it even. Besides, you don't have a job yet."

"As far as calling it even, that's not something you should worry about. Besides, if that were the case, then you'd have more than made up for it. You're right about the job though. I'll need one pretty soon, but I'm not broke yet so let me pitch in my share."

Jess chuckled, "Funny, I don't remember you being such an 'onry cuss. Okay then, you can help out with the groceries."

"Is that all?" Tandon was surprised, then he laughed, "By the time I'm done feeding you you'll wish you'd suggested something else."

Jess laughed too. "We'll just have to get the team together and play some ball. That should keep us in shape."

Tandon said he was looking forward to that.

"My folks had mentioned something about hiring on another hand at their feed store after the hearing at the end of the month," Jess said. "In case you're interested."

"Thanks. I'll keep it in mind," Tandon said, grateful for the suggestion and also grateful to JulieAnn's family for their willingness to accept him into their lives.

That very day Tandon had packed what few belongings he had, which weren't much, just some basic toiletries and the week's worth of clothes he had brought with him, and after stopping at the hotel desk to sign out, climbed into his borrowed truck and headed to Jess' where he would spend the next four weeks, when they weren't out doing their own things, getting to know each other better. It wasn't long before Tandon came to see Jess as the brother he always wanted. And that made what he was planning even better.

* * *

JulieAnn felt as if she had hit the happiness

jackpot. Every day the blessings just kept pouring in. She felt like the luckiest woman in the world, and it showed. From the moment she woke until she finally fell asleep she exuded a sparkling zest for life. From her ever present smile to her tuneless but joyful whistling and humming, from her spontaneous and uninhibited flouncing through rooms to her enthusiasm for any and all tasks, whether involved or mundane, JulieAnn's spirits could not be contained.

That the man she loved was back in her life, something she had never foreseen happening again, and that she could freely immerse herself in their relationship because of the support of her family, made her someone she almost didn't recognize. She remembered, for a moment, another time when she had felt nearly this good, but had quickly dismissed the memory because that time it had not ended well. But this was so different. She knew, with unfailing conviction, that this was it. They had weathered their storms and had come out on top. Now nothing could separate them again.

There was only one downside to their days together, and that was the time they had to be apart. It was the first time she had regretted her job, knowing that every minute spent working was another minute missed with Tandon. But she had learned to compensate for that. She daydreamed. Sometimes her thoughts were centered on Tandon alone and other times she focused on their shared moments together. No matter what she was doing Tandon was never out of her mind. On one occasion, though, that had almost gotten her into trouble. She hadn't been aware she'd been doing anything out of the ordinary at work until one day.

"JulieAnn?" She hushed. She had been humming various tunes by her favorite singer when she heard Rebecca speak from the next room. "Are you finished with the articles?"

"Oh, sure." JulieAnn got up from her desk and walked over to another table where she had lain the articles after editing them. "Here you go," she said and handed them to Rebecca with a smile.

Five minutes later, JulieAnn heard Rebecca start to giggle. She just smiled to herself, not even looking up as she continued humming and working. It wasn't until Rebecca's giggle had turned into full blown laughter that she finally swiveled her chair around to face her friend.

JulieAnn couldn't help but chuckle as she asked, "What's so funny?" For some reason that set Rebecca to laughing even harder, if that were possible. By now tears were streaming down Rebecca's face and she was doubled over, holding her sides. Unable to get a word out, she simply thumped her finger onto the table, pointing to the object of her hilarity.

Curious, JulieAnn stood up and walked over. Rebecca had begun separating the articles into different piles, but the place she had pointed to still had the unsorted pieces strewn about like a spilled deck of cards. It took a moment for her to spot the culprit. Then she gasped. Her face grew warmer and warmer until it was fairly steaming with embarrassment. When had she done that…and how could she not have noticed? Quickly, she snatched up the paper and held it to her chest.

That set Rebecca into another fit, but after she calmed down a bit, and only a bit, she said, "Don't worry. I think everyone's probably done that at one time or another."

JulieAnn couldn't resist taking another look. She pulled the paper from her, then grimaced. It was all right there in black and white - or rather, red and white. It was obvious from her red ink marks on the paper that she had begun, with good intentions, to make her corrections to the article. But somewhere, in the midst of her concentration, her mind had begun to wander.

The article was a serious one. A citizen's response to a previous one written by the mayor. At the end of one of the paragraphs JulieAnn had drawn a line out to the margin, presumably to make a note, but instead she had copied down her thoughts verbatim.

She read it. "Tandon, Tandon, wherefore art thou Tandon?" Oh brother, she thought dismayed, then read on. "Brown thrush singing all day long in the leaves above me, take my love this April song, 'Love me, love me, love me!' When he harkens what you say, bid him, lest he miss me, 'Leave his work or leave his play, and kiss me, kiss me, kiss me!'" And the last demands were in large, capitalized letters and heavily underlined. It was the "Love Me" poem by her favorite poet, Sara Teasdale. JulieAnn slapped the paper to her chest again and groaned, wondering when she had become such a sap.

Rebecca choked back her laughter to ask,

"Would you like me to work that into the column or would you prefer I place it in the personals?"

JulieAnn looked up at Rebecca and saw the merriment dancing in her eyes. Seeing her friend's teasing face, JulieAnn couldn't resist any longer and began laughing. It was good to be able to laugh with Rebecca. She had worried the night before she was to go back to work, after her week off, what Rebecca's reaction would be to her on-again relationship with Tandon. In actuality, it wasn't so much that as it was the concern for her friend over her plans to set her brother and her up.

Rebecca had treated her even more affectionately, more sisterly, in the hope, perhaps even presumption, that her set-up would work. And for that reason, and out of respect for Rebecca, JulieAnn's first task when she returned to the office was to talk to her and tell her what had happened and hope that she wouldn't be too disappointed.

"Good morning Becca," she began as she normally would have.

Rebecca greeted her with a warm hug and an eager look. "Hey! How was your vacation? I can't believe I haven't talked to you all week."

JulieAnn set her bag down feeling a bit guilty. Lately, well since Marshall had moved there, they'd been talking steadily, nearly every day. Even on weekends they managed to either visit with each other or gab on the phone, and with much more frequency than they had in the past. But the week prior, she knew, she hadn't given Rebecca a single thought so preoccupied was she with her own life. And now she was sorry about that, though Rebecca appeared unconcerned about it. For now.

"Sorry about that. I was really busy last week."

"I'd say so. I must have called you a dozen times. I even stopped by, but you were gone then too."

JulieAnn smiled warily, "I was out of town most of the time."

"Oh yeah? Where'd you go?" Rebecca asked, looking genuinely interested.

JulieAnn looked at Rebecca and swallowed, shrugging, "Eureka Springs and a few places in Missouri."

For some reason JulieAnn felt as if she was keeping a secret, and that was not at all what she intended. "Look, Rebecca," JulieAnn said, then pulled out her chair while grabbing one for Rebecca who wordlessly complied as she faced JulieAnn. "I know you've had this idea that Marshall and I...well, become a couple. And," she rushed on not wanting her friend to feel bad for trying, "it may have happened eventually...he's a great guy, but," she took a deep breath, feeling the need to sugar coat what she wanted to say, but she didn't quite know how, so she decided to just be direct. "Tandon's back. That's who I was with all week."

JulieAnn didn't say anything more as she waited, watching Rebecca's face trying to figure out what she might be thinking.

Rebecca leaned back in her chair and with arms crossed, smiled. "I was wondering when you'd get around to telling me."

JulieAnn could only look at her, puzzled.

"I already know about the two of you,"

Rebecca said.

"You do?"

Rebecca explained, "I was worried about you since I couldn't get a hold of you, so I called Jess. He told me everything."

Why hadn't she considered that before? Of course her brother would have said something. JulieAnn looked apologetic as she said, "You should have heard about it from me."

"Oh, don't worry about it. I understand," Rebecca said with a smile.

JulieAnn tried to read between the lines, if indeed there was anything to read at all. She wondered whether Rebecca was trying to feign her matter-of-fact attitude or if, in fact, she really did understand. "What about…?"

"Marshall?" Rebecca knew what was on JulieAnn's mind. "I've explained everything to him as well. He understands the chemistry between you two. There's no hard feelings," she said with a wave of her hand.

JulieAnn sighed then, relieved with the outcome of the conversation. She guessed she'd been worried for nothing. It seemed that since Marshall was okay with it Rebecca would also be okay with it.

JulieAnn clapped her palms onto her lap and smiled, "Well then, I better get some work done," and they had both stood to begin the work day.

* * *

It was nearing four o'clock that afternoon as JulieAnn and Rebecca began closing down for the day when the bell's jingling on the door sounded.

JulieAnn was in the back and she smiled, knowing who it was. "I'll be right out," she said.

It took her only a few moments to finish what she was doing, but the time seemed interminably slow as she tried to hurry along. She heard voices, then, and relaxed a bit. Rebecca would keep him company until she could get out there.

When she had finally finished and had shut the machines off, JulieAnn eagerly stepped around the corner to greet Tandon with an enthusiastic smile only to stop short at the sight before her. She inhaled deeply. Not only was Tandon standing there, but Marshall too.

Something strange happened to her at that moment. Something she couldn't quite grasp.

The men were standing only a few steps from one another, yet it seemed, as she looked at them, as if the two were separated by a great divide. As if two different worlds, each having their own uniqueness, were being offered to her. Images of each man's actions and personalities snapped before her like a children's book Daniel had once shown her where the corners of the pages were drawn in sequence and as you flipped quickly through them you would see the character's movements. But it was the differences between them that she was seeing now.

"We were just telling Tandon how happy we were for you both," Rebecca said, waking JulieAnn from her stupor.

Everyone was looking at her, waiting. Purposely, she pushed her thoughts away and smiled, "Thank you." Then she faced the two men. "So, you've met?"

Tandon had walked around her desk to stand beside her and put his arm around her. "Rebecca introduced us."

There was silence, then Tandon began, "If you're finished here…"

"Oh, yes. I'm ready." JulieAnn looked from Rebecca to Marshall, both of whom wore smiles. They were the same as when she'd rounded the corner. JulieAnn grabbed her bag as they passed by her desk on the way to the door. She turned then, "Bye. See you tomorrow Becca." She looked at Marshall then. "It was good seeing you again." He only nodded.

A moment later, while riding away with Tandon, JulieAnn realized that Marshall hadn't said one word to her. And he hadn't hugged her.

CHAPTER TWENTY

It was the twenty-fifth of October and the afternoon's autumn air was unusually blistery…numbing, as it blew in from the open window.

Tandon had turned the truck's heater off about twenty miles back, opting for shock therapy in a desperate need to distract himself from a case of the nerves. Somehow, he had figured that freezing would do the trick. But it didn't.

He was on his way to see JulieAnn. It would be the last chance they would have to spend some quality time together for several days. Tomorrow morning she would be leaving on the bus to Washington, and though he planned to see her off, it wouldn't be until after the meeting on the twenty-eighth that he would see her again. And if everything he was planning went the way he hoped, it would make their time apart seem that much longer.

As he pried his locked fingers from the wheel to steer the truck, hand over hand, into JulieAnn's driveway, he noticed he was shivering. Great strategy, he thought, feeling foolish now. Before he could maneuver his frigid limbs out of the truck he heard a screen door bang shut, then JulieAnn's footsteps as she neared.

"Hey, just the man I was looking for," she said then stopped, standing just inside his opened door. She took one look at his cherry red nose, the rosy blotches on his cheeks, his watering eyes, and chapped lips, and gasped.

As Tandon turned his gaze toward her, he noticed her surprise turn quickly to humor.

A giggle escaped her throat. "You look like a combination between a clown and old St. Nicholas." She leaned in and gave him a kiss then yelped, jumping back. "You really are cold," she said with all seriousness. She looked over to the passenger seat, then scolded him. "What good is your jacket if you don't wear it?"

She leaned over him then and grabbed his jacket. Despite the fact that the open door was making him even colder, Tandon managed to smile, enjoying this never before seen clucking and fussing from JulieAnn.

"Typical man. You'd all rather look cool and macho than to wear a hat and coat." Reaching around him she opened his jacket to lay its quilted interior across his back, pulling the front sides forward, hugging him. "Didn't you have the heater on?" she asked.

At his silence she glanced at him, then did a

double take. Misreading his expression, she exclaimed, "It doesn't work? Well, you can't drive around all winter without heat. We'll go in and call Jess and have him come over and fix it right now."

Tandon spoke then knowing that if he didn't she would do just that. "No, the heater works just fine."

A confused crease dimpled her brows. "Well, why didn't you turn it on then?" she asked.

He couldn't tell her the truth. That might give too much away. He had no choice but to tell a little white lie. "I'd had a long day. I thought the fresh air might wake me up."

She looked at him oddly. "Did it work?"

Tandon forced his facial muscles into his cheeriest smile. "You bet! And just as soon as I'm thawed we can get started."

JulieAnn stepped back as Tandon slid his body out of the seat. "Oh we can, can we?" she said with a sly look and tilt of her head. "You sound like you have a plan up your sleeve."

He ignored her obvious meaning. "I do," he said, matter-of-fact like and stepped to the back of the truck concealing a grin. Pulling a, thankfully, lightweight box from the bed, he announced with a shake of the contents, "Halloween decorations."

JulieAnn let out a gusty laugh as they turned to head into the house. "I usually just hand out candy to the kids."

Tandon stepped aside so JulieAnn could open the door for him. "This time, we'll do it in style."

* * *

JulieAnn couldn't keep the knot from

tightening in her stomach. She knew she was probably being foolish. She didn't even, really, have a reason for it, but it was there all the same. As she rubbed the soapy dish cloth over their dinner plates and rinsed them, she watched Tandon covertly as he removed and opened the decorations in the living room.

She had thought she'd been simply imagining things...earlier, when she'd gone to meet him outside. The condition he had arrived in had definitely floored her, and what he said, well, it was more about what he hadn't said. It felt like he was keeping something from her.

She was just putting away the last of their dishes when Tandon called to her to come see what he had brought. After hanging her damp towel on a bar to dry, she stepped through the doorway and gasped. Her once tidy living room was now strewn in a colorful disarray of tornadic proportion. There was a very real looking skeleton draped across one chair while another had two costumes lying on it. They were a coordinating set of Sonny and Cher. She had to laugh at that. "You're too big to be Sonny."

"Who said anything about me being Sonny?" They both chuckled.

There was fake webbing to be hung, hordes of cheap trinkets and treasures...every child's dream, and all over the floor were opened bags of candy in every sweet concoction known to man. And sitting in the midst of all this chaos was Tandon, and in his lap - a pumpkin piñata, which besides snagging pieces for himself, he was stuffing full to the brim with the sugary assortment.

"You know," she began, curious to hear this explanation, "usually you put candy in the trick-or-treaters bags, then they run off to the next house." She raised her brows at the piñata.

Tandon grinned at her. "And the tradition will live on. This guy, however," he patted the pumpkin's head, "has bigger plans."

"Oh, he does, does he?"

"Yes, he does." Merriment danced in his eyes. "I was thinking, if it's all right with you of course..." She grinned at his obvious hesitation. "That we could throw a Halloween party here."

JulieAnn was immediately taken with the idea. "That's a great idea Tandon! Oh, how fun!"

"I was hoping you'd think so. I thought Anna and John, if they don't think they're too old, and your nephews would like a piñata."

"Oh, of course! They'd love it." She spun around clasping her hands together, her mind already at work. "We'll need more decorations. Oh, I saw a house last year with straw bundled together and tied against posts. We need to do that. And games. We can bob for apples," she turned around pointing, "beat the piñata...oh, and offer food. I'll have to make caramel apples, my apple pies, hot apple cider..." She bit her thumbnail, "Oh, that's a lot of apples."

She stopped then at the sound of Tandon's laughter and watched him as he picked himself off of the floor and came to her wrapping her in his arms.

"Slow down there lady. I'm glad you're so

excited, but don't go putting too much on your plate. Remember, you're leaving tomorrow for Washington and won't be back until the night before Halloween. You might want to get your family to pitch in."

"I'd almost forgotten. You're right." Excitedly, she twisted herself out of his embrace, "I should call everyone and let them know. They'll want to…"

"Hold on there," Tandon laughed, grabbing the back of her shirt as she turned to head to the kitchen phone. "First things first." He got behind her and held her upper arms, steering her toward his vacated spot on the floor. "How about we finish the decorating and, while we're doing that, we can think more about the plans. Here," he nudged her down, "you can finish filling the piñata while I run out to the truck and get more supplies." He bent down and kissed the top of her head.

JulieAnn tipped her head up. In her excitement she had forgotten all about her earlier worries, but now they returned in full force. "Oh? I don't remember seeing anything else." There was only a second's pause, but to JulieAnn it was very distinctive.

"No? Well, I must have covered it. Sorry."

She noticed as he apologized to the floor that something had changed. He seemed distracted.

The next moment he bent down and pulled an opened bag of candy out from under the chair. "Here it is. I thought there was another bag." He handed it over to JulieAnn. "This should fill the rest of the piñata."

JulieAnn frowned. There was still candy lying

all over the floor that she could have used.

"Fill it good now. I'll be back in a minute."

JulieAnn watched him as he walked away not quite knowing what to think. Something was definitely not right. She was tempted to follow him and see what he was up to but decided against such tactics. She felt bad enough with her thoughts as they were. Pushing the doubts aside, she set the piñata in her lap, popped a piece of the candy into her mouth, and dove into her job, her thoughts returning to the party planning.

* * *

It was dark now as Tandon stepped outside. The temperature had dropped some and he rubbed his arms as he hurried to the truck. This time it was merely due to forgetfulness that he wasn't wearing his coat, but as it turned out, a very welcome mental block.

The dome light came on in the truck as he opened the door. As he reached out his arm he stopped, looking back at the house to make sure JulieAnn wasn't watching from the window. Not seeing her, he turned back too quickly and hit his forehead on the door frame. He let out a throaty growl and lifted his hand to his head. The only thing he felt was sweat so he hastily wiped his sleeved arm across his face. Then, as he reached his hand to the glove compartment, he felt more sweat, a bead of it, trickling down the center of his back. Great, he thought as he wriggled, pulling on his shirt at the same time.

While he'd planned for this night in the weeks prior he'd been nothing short of excited. It had been a true test of his stamina to act normal around JulieAnn when all the time he wanted to jump and shout for joy, but he'd had to tame his inner child. Even the difficulties of deciding which day to do it on and what he would say, even the time-consuming shopping with its own issues over which style would be most loved hadn't dampened his enthusiasm.

But now that the moment was here he felt all hands as he pulled the white box out. He opened it quickly, just to be sure it was there, nearly dropping it as he snapped the lid shut, then turned around closing the truck's door. He knew it wasn't the most creative idea in the world, his plan, but it was all he could come up with that he was sure hadn't been tried by countless other hopeful men in similar situations. Hurrying, before he missed his moment, he ran up the steps, then calmed himself with a deep breath before entering quietly.

* * *

JulieAnn giggled like a naughty little girl when she realized she was eating more of the candy than she was putting in the piñata. "Okay, this is the last one," she ordered herself and popped a creamy milk chocolate Hershey's Kiss into her mouth. She closed her eyes for a moment, as she sucked on it, savoring the smooth taste of a treat she rarely thought to have. Finally finishing it, she decided she had poked around long enough. It was time to finish the job. Picking up the end of the bag she dumped the rest of the kisses onto the floor and set the empty package in the box with the other trash.

As she moved to grab a handful of the candy,

she stopped, her hand hovering, as her attention was drawn to one unusual piece. The paper flag that opens the silver foil was not the same as the others. In fact, this one was not paper. It wasn't white and it didn't have the Hershey name written on it. This one was red, and cloth. It was a ribbon. Perplexed, she picked it up, then looked back down at the others. No, this was the only one like it.

Suddenly, it occurred to her that Tandon had done this. She smiled at the thought. She would never have guessed that he'd take the time to do something so...sweet. She chuckled, then decided she couldn't hurt his feelings by not eating it, so she pulled on the ribbon. But it was not chocolate that fell into her palm. It was a ring. Surprised, she picked it up and studied it, a curious grin spreading across her face. It was a trinket, a child's toy ring with an expandable slit in the band and a piece of red plastic for the "jewel". She laughed then, realizing she'd seen these in the ten cent bubble gum machines. She slid it onto her pinky and held her hand up, admiring it as if it were real when Tandon's voice behind her startled her.

"I can have it sized if it doesn't fit."

JulieAnn turned quickly with a little squeal and caught the mischievous look in his eye. She jumped up and went to him. "You're so sneaky. How did you come up with this?" She kissed his cheek, still grinning broadly.

"Well, actually," she waited as he paused, looking at her, then took a step back while at the same time taking her hands in his, "I think I can do one better."

The next moment, as JulieAnn watched, Tandon bent down on one knee, then let go of one hand to dig into his back pocket only to bring it back to the startled gasp of the woman before him.

The silly emotions she felt a moment ago had been markedly replaced as she stood there, now dumbstruck.

"JulieAnn," Tandon began, his voice soft, "we've known each other all of our lives. We grew up in the same town, went to the same school, were playmates as kids, and later, high school sweethearts. Even the years we were apart, we were together." Tandon gave her hand a squeeze. "You've given me so much JulieAnn - your love, your support, your faith. And you've taught me how to do the same."

Tears were flowing down JulieAnn's face and she struggled to swallow as her throat constricted with emotion.

"You never gave up on us, not once, despite all the reasons I gave you to. JulieAnn, I want to spend the rest of my life making up for my mistakes. I want to earn your love and your respect. And I want to prove to you every day that you've made the right decision." Tandon let go of her hand then to clasp the box with both hands as she took that opportunity to swipe her hand across her wet face, to no avail. The look she saw in his eyes as he looked back at her made her knees nearly buckle and her tears to flow again.

"JulieAnn, I want to honor you and cherish you, protect you and care for you…and love you for the rest of my life." JulieAnn watched as Tandon slowly opened the white box, then gasped at the ring that winked back at her. "Will you marry me?"

JulieAnn looked through the blur of tears to the boy, the man, that she had always loved with all of her heart and nodded, choking on tears of joy and falling to her knees, whispering hoarsely, "Yes. Yes, I'll marry you."

CHAPTER TWENTY-ONE

That night was the first night Tandon and JulieAnn remained together. Newly engaged, and knowing JulieAnn would be leaving the next morning, the couple didn't want to separate so Tandon stayed. There was nothing on this earth that was going to ruin their special wedding day, however, and they both, with unvoiced agreement, kept guard of their emotions.

To occupy their time and busy their thoughts they drank coffee and ate JulieAnn's homemade cherry pie and a midnight breakfast all the while kissing and cuddling and making plans for their future. They talked about the kind of wedding they'd like to have and quickly agreed to a simple country wedding with family and friends at her grandparents homestead. They knew Grandmother Annabelle would love it. They discussed life's ironies, how things could change just like that. That included themselves as well as others such as

Tandon's father and the fact that Isaac Bowman would be at his son's wedding. They talked about the Halloween party and how it would be the perfect time to announce their engagement. The last subject they pushed aside until it was too close to ignore…how excruciatingly painful it will be to be apart from one another. Even if for only a few days.

The hours passed quickly, too quickly, and before they knew it, it was six a.m. and they were at the court house loading JulieAnn's suitcase onto the bus. Everyone was there. The people chosen to speak, JulieAnn who would be recording the event, and Marshall, who had volunteered to drive the bus. Supporters were there too lending their encouragement. The air was buzzing with excitement.

As Tandon steered JulieAnn to the table that someone had graciously set up with steaming cups of coffee and fresh bakery, JulieAnn asked for the umpteenth time, "You're sure you don't want to go?"

"No," he answered with a chuckle, "I'd rather not, but I'll see you after the meeting. You have my apartment number right?"

"Here, in my purse," JulieAnn said and patted her bag.

"Good."

"Hey, JulieAnn," Becca came over, bumping through the crowd, "we should get some group shots before you go."

"You're right," JulieAnn looked apologetically at Tandon, "Sorry."

"I understand. Go ahead."

JulieAnn pulled her camera from her bag and handed it to Becca. "Here, you can do the honors." And with a quick kiss for Tandon, JulieAnn led Becca away.

After a few minutes Tandon heard an unseen voice announce that group pictures were being set up on the side of the bus. He got jostled back a few times as folks made their way forward, and noticing a few skeptical looks as they passed, began to feel a bit awkward.

"Tandon." He turned, and seeing Jess heading toward him, relaxed his shoulders.

"Hi."

"Exciting, huh?" Jess said with a friendly pat on the back.

"Sure."

"Jul's seems to be having fun," Jess pointed to the group being photographed when JulieAnn, standing among them, picked that moment to look over at Tandon and make a playful kissing gesture. They both laughed when they saw the camera flash at that moment.

"You want to say hi to the family?" Jess asked. "They're over there," he said, pointing in their direction.

"I will in a bit. I want to see JulieAnn off first."

"Oh, right," Jess said with a broad wink.

"Ah, get out of here," Tandon chuckled, playfully pushing him away.

As Jess headed away there was another loud announcement for everyone to say their goodbyes. The bus was leaving in ten minutes.

Tandon's eyes sought out JulieAnn and saw her

making her way to her family. He waited patiently, drinking down his coffee, watching her hug everyone. The thought came to him, not for the first time, how nice it must be to have such a large loving family. Then he grinned like a man satisfied. Soon, very soon, he'd become a part of this family. His wife's family. He liked the sound of that. His wife.

"Tandon," JulieAnn said.

He blinked.

"What are you grinning about?" she asked, mimicking his own expression.

"Oh, nothing."

Looking offended that he wouldn't tell her, she pouted, "Well, you sure get happy about nothing."

Tandon laughed at that, pulling her into his arms. With his mouth to her ear, he whispered, "I was thinking about the day we say, 'I do.'"

JulieAnn pulled back in his arms to see his face. Apparently satisfied she pulled him into a tight embrace. "I'm going to miss you," she whispered.

"Me too," he said emotionally.

"I know it's only for two days, but," she couldn't finish.

"I know," he said understandingly, then pulled back, "but just think, this time next week I'll have moved here for good, our families will know we're engaged, and we can plan the day that we've waited for all our lives." He kissed her. "Then we'll never be apart again." JulieAnn smiled through happy tears, stood on her toes, and kissed him back.

That unseen voice shouted again, this time, that it was time to go.

With a last kiss and a wave to her family, Tandon watched as JulieAnn boarded the bus, then taking a window seat, slid down the top half of the window and snapped pictures of the crowd and him. After a few short moments the bus pulled away. Tandon waved, along with everyone else, but with his interest in only one cause.

Walking back to the truck with his mind on JulieAnn, Tandon only half heard JulieAnn's father say, as he came up and patted him on the back, "Glad you two are together again," then Jess when he walked by him with a quick, "Good thing you changed your mind or we might have had a riot on our hands," and laughed.

With distracted nods to both, Tandon drove away, hoping the next two days would pass quickly.

* * *

Nothing could bring people together better than a passion for the same cause. That became evident over the next several hours as the bus became a blur of voices as everyone discussed the upcoming meeting. It became so loud at one point that JulieAnn began to worry about Marshall. She was sure the volume and all the different discussions must be distracting him from his driving, but when she looked to the front of the bus she saw that he too was caught up in a conversation.

Marshall looked into the rear view mirror, then, and caught her grinning at him but quickly averted his gaze as if caught in an unseemly act. Frustrated, JulieAnn made a mental note to end this awkwardness and talk to him. To let him know they could still be friends. But that would have to wait for another time and a less public place. For now she had other things to distract her.

When the trip began JulieAnn, ever the reporter, had had pen and paper ready and waiting for any tidbit of information, but she soon gave that up. She decided to just enjoy the trip and the people. This was, in fact, her first real trip out of Arkansas and she wanted to take it all in.

After a while, when the conversations dwindled down, she was able to spend some time gazing out the window. They passed through some good sized cities. They were larger than she was used to, but not intimidatingly so. She didn't mind them, but was happy when the fields, with their crops and cattle, became visible again. Guess I'm just a country girl at heart, she thought with a smile. Watching the scenery go by was having a hypnotic effect on her, not to mention the lack of sleep the night before, and before she knew it, she had fallen asleep.

* * *

Weary from the day long drive JulieAnn washed her face, reapplied a light touch of makeup, and combed her hair. Before the group had gotten off the bus that evening they had decided that, after an hour of getting settled and changed, they would meet in the hotel lobby and go together to a nice restaurant. Despite their long day they were eager to get out and see the sites.

JulieAnn was just clasping her shoe strap and planning to call Tandon when there was a knock at the door. With a glance at the phone, she stepped to the door and opened it.

"Hi, JulieAnn."

JulieAnn's heart leapt. "Hi, Marshall."

Marshall cleared his throat before going on, "The group is starting to gather in the lobby. I thought you might…"

"Oh, I'm ready. Let me get my purse." As she turned away, she remembered her earlier intentions to talk to him and turned around. "Marshall, would you come in for just a moment, please." She watched as he looked uncomfortably down one side of the hall to the next, then stepped in leaving the door open. She had to look away for a moment to suppress a sudden giggle that threatened her.

"Marshall, this has got to stop." She saw his partly surprised, partly guilty, look. "You and I have been friends from day one. We were comfortable with each other the first time we met so I don't understand why you're so uncomfortable around me now." Then she conceded, "No, that's not true. I do know why. It's because I'm with Tandon." There, she said it. She knows he knows, but now it's out in the open between them.

"I know Becca told you how far back we go and the situation with us." She noticed he kept his gaze down. Although things had never really gone anywhere between them, she felt like she was breaking his heart, and it tore at hers.

"Marshall," she wanted him to look at her. Finally, after a moment, he did. "I didn't know he was coming back. If he hadn't, things might have…" she had to stop herself. She shook her head and looked at him, "But that doesn't mean we can't be friends. I want to be friends with you," she said, meaning it.

JulieAnn was actually surprised at how deeply his feelings for her had actually gone. His goofiness before Tandon came back had not been any indicator, and now she was not only surprised, but deeply touched. And, she knew that, had Tandon not come back that she probably would have fallen in love with Marshall, eventually.

"Well," she said, smiling and taking a step toward him, "what do you say? Friends?" She could almost see his mind turning it over.

After a moment a grin began spreading across his face and a twinkle came back into his eyes. "Friends is fine with me," he said cheerily.

"Good. I'm glad." she said and moved to hug him, but he turned and held the door open.

"Ready to get something to eat?"

"Sure."

When she reached up to turn off the lights she saw her ring twinkle and told herself she'd call Tandon later.

Marshall followed her out, shutting the door behind them.

CHAPTER TWENTY-TWO

Tandon had been back in his apartment for an hour when the phone rang. He smiled knowingly, "Hello?"

"Hello, fiancé," came the sweet reply.

Tandon laughed, "I like the sound of that, but I'll like husband even more." JulieAnn chuckled. "You sound tired," he said.

"I am. Oh, Tandon, I'm sorry I didn't reach you last night. We got in late, then went out for dinner. I was so tired when I got back, I just fell asleep."

Tandon smiled, "That's okay. I figured as much."

"Thanks. I think we're going to have a repeat of it again tonight. I'll have to turn in early so I'm alert tomorrow for the meeting."

"I understand. How was the trip otherwise?"

"Oh, it was so beautiful. Tandon, you have to promise me that we'll take lots of trips and see this beautiful country we live in."

He laughed, "I promise. Maybe I should add it to my vows."

She laughed too. "Hey, enough talk about me, how was your flight? How much packing have you done?"

He laughed again, "The flight was nice, and are you hoping to get out of helping me?"

"Not on your life," she said, then yawned.

"Okay, I heard that. I'll let you go."

"I miss you."

"I miss you too," he said. "I'll see you tomorrow."

"Bright eyed and bushy tailed."

"I love you, JulieAnn."

"I love you too, Tandon."

* * *

Tandon was still chuckling about his conversation with JulieAnn half an hour later as he grabbed his apartment keys to go downstairs and get some moving boxes. He was just closing his door when he heard his name and turned.

"Greg!" he said, surprised.

Greg Zimmerman closed the distance between them and the two shook hands. "How are you, Tandon?"

"Good sir," he answered. "How are you?"

"I'm fine, just fine." After a thoughtful moment Greg gestured toward the door, "Can we go in and talk?"

Tandon jumped to obey, "Of course," he said and reopened the door.

Tandon saw Greg observing the clutter lying around the room. "I'm moving," he explained simply, then offered him the recliner and took a seat opposite him on the couch.

"So, Tandon," Greg began, "have you enjoyed your time off?"

Tandon thought Greg's wording sounded a bit odd, but he ignored it. "Yes, I have." A big smile spread across his face, "As a matter of fact, you can congratulate me. I'm getting married."

"Well, that's wonderful. Congratulations." Greg stood up and reached across to pat Tandon on the back and shake his hand. "Let me guess," he said as they sat back down, "she's the one who had you moping around when you got back from Arkansas?"

Tandon gave him a sheepish grin and chuckled, "She's the one."

"She must be very special."

Tandon smiled, picturing JulieAnn, "Yes, she sure is."

Silence filled the room then and he wondered why Greg was there.

Greg straightened then, becoming business-like, and turned to pick up the manila folder he had carried in. Without a word he handed it to Tandon. Something about this unnerved him. He opened the folder hesitantly and looked at the paper before him, bewilderment creasing his brow. It was his resignation.

He looked up at Greg, confused. "Why did you give me this?" he asked.

Greg shifted slightly, "I never filed it."

Tandon didn't understand, "Why not?"

"Well, a couple of reasons really."

Under Tandon's quizzical stare he explained, "For one, I knew you loved your job too much to really want to quit." Greg put his hand up when Tandon opened his mouth to reply. "Please." Greg went on. "Sometimes we just get stressed and overwhelmed and need a good old fashioned break," he paused. "So, I gave you one."

"A break?"

"A leave of absence."

Tandon frowned. This was all just too much. "You mean I'm still employed?"

Greg nodded, "With the same pay and benefits."

Tandon was speechless. He stood up abruptly and walked to the large picture window overlooking the view of the city streets and park below. He was frustrated, and not a little irritated, at the notion that Greg hadn't taken his resignation seriously. He was sure he meant well, but... Tandon sighed, running his hand through his hair and turned around to tell him just that.

"Look, Greg, I know..."

Greg stood up suddenly and interrupted him, "Tandon, there's something else." The two looked at one another. "I need you at the meeting tomorrow."

"What? No!" Tandon took a step back, stunned by Greg's ridiculous words. He shook his head, "Greg, I resigned. I'm sorry you misunderstood, but I don't work for you anymore."

"We need your testimony," Greg said firmly.

"Why? You have my files."

Greg threw his hands up, dismissing the

thought. "That's just paperwork," then looked hard at Tandon, "We need *you* there, in person."

Tandon looked at Greg, his eyes narrowing with his thoughts, "Is this why you chose me to go to Arkansas? Was this part of your plan? Why didn't you mention it before?"

Now it was Greg who moved to the window. Frustrated, he faced Tandon, "No, there was no plan. We sent you there for the reasons we told you, to help the landowners understand our position."

Tandon nodded, "And now, because that didn't work, you want me to go to the House meeting to help them understand." Tandon frowned at Greg, "I thought the Park Service was confident about getting the river. Has something happened?"

"No, no," Greg waved his hand dismissively and looked out the window, "We know it's in the bag."

"Then why the extra precautions?" Tandon studied Greg closely. Several long minutes passed as he waited, looking at the back of Greg's head.

Finally, with a heavy sigh, Greg mumbled, seemingly more to himself than to Tandon, "It's politics."

Tandon knew then that this was something to do with Greg, and he knew too that he would get nothing more from him. Something about Greg's stance tore at him, and after berating himself for what he was about to do, he said reluctantly, "Alright, I'll go," and shook his head irritated with his own foolishness.

Greg faced him, taking a deep breath, and Tandon could see how much his answer meant to him. "Thank you, Tandon." Greg walked over to him and shook his hand firmly, "Thank you."

"You're welcome."

Briefly, Greg went over what time to be there and where to meet before he left looking relieved, and leaving Tandon still curious as to the story he left untold.

"Oh," he said aloud, and took a few steps toward the door before stopping. He wanted to tell Greg to be sure and submit his resignation after the meeting, but decided he could just tell him tomorrow after the meeting.

On the heels of that thought came thoughts of JulieAnn. Well, she would be surprised, he was certain. She had asked him numerous times if he wanted to go to the meeting and he had insisted that he did not, and yet, here he was now planning to go.

Suddenly he became nervous at the thought. This was a big deal. A huge deal. He, Tandon Bowman, was going to go before the members of the House Subcommittee on National Parks and Recreation. He suddenly felt a little queasy. He needed to distract himself.

He went to the kitchen and sat down with the phone. JulieAnn would definitely find this whole incident funny. The line rang numerous times, but she never answered. Then he remembered they were all going out to eat. He made a mental note to try her in the morning and went downstairs for those boxes. He had packing to do.

* * *

After returning to her hotel room after dinner, JulieAnn called Jess to let the family know she had made it safe and sound to D.C. They, in turn, had strict instructions for her to bring back as much information as possible. They wanted to know exactly what was said. That was a tall order, she laughed.

After a few more minutes she hung up, exhausted, and opened her suitcase for her nightgown. Beneath it was a large envelope. She took it out, smiling. She had meant to give it to Tandon the night before she left, but he had distracted her with his surprise proposal. She decided she would give it to him tomorrow after the meeting. She walked over to her reporting bag and put it in there where she wouldn't forget it. She would bring it with her to his apartment and surprise him with it there. She realized it was silly to have brought it on the trip when he was just going to have to bring it back with him anyway, but she couldn't wait any longer. She had waited, and sometimes forgotten, long enough.

Finally, with a prayer of thanksgiving and to ask for His hand over the proceedings the following day, JulieAnn fell into a peaceful sleep.

CHAPTER TWENTY-THREE

The outside of the House of Representatives was a mass of moving bodies with a full schedule of meetings set for the day. How was he ever going to find Greg Zimmerman, let alone his fiancée, in this throng, he wondered. Tandon had tried to get in touch with JulieAnn this morning but managed to miss her again. Now, unaware he was coming, the effort to meet would be his alone.

Finally, Tandon spotted his group with their distinctive Park uniforms and headed in their direction. He walked up behind Greg and put his hand on his shoulder so that he turned.

"Tandon, thanks for coming," Greg said, relief evident in his voice.

Tandon merely smiled, then greeted the others. He turned then to search for the group from Arkansas among the dizzying crowd and finally spotted her. She was taking a picture of a lady in their group. He smiled. He should have guessed, he thought, humored. He was about to walk over when the announcement went out and Greg steered Tandon around to follow them. He didn't mind though. He knew he would see her inside.

There was a certain seating arrangement and everyone was quickly ushered to their prearranged areas. The room was so much more in person than in photographs, Tandon thought, as he looked around in awe. It was very expansive with its high ceiling and curved seating arrangement. He felt very dignified just by being in the room and knowing so many important men and women throughout history had stood in there.

When everyone was seated the meeting began with the chairman announcing the bill and introducing the groups and individuals participating. As he had done with the other introductions, Tandon let his gaze roam across the room until, at the mention of her group, it came to rest on JulieAnn. He couldn't help but smile. She looked beautiful sitting there, her demeanor very proper and business-like as she tried to portray professionalism. But Tandon preferred, far more, what he saw as the down to earth woman he loved. He couldn't help but remember that night, over a year ago, when at another meeting he saw her sitting in a crowd ready to report on this very subject. An unexpected shiver ran through him then, and he stiffened.

Finally, the last of the introductions were made and all eyes turned politely in their direction. The Park Service team faced the chairman respectfully at their mention, then relaxed. Then Tandon turned to face JulieAnn. Seeing the blood drain from her face, Tandon wished now that he had made a better attempt to reach her before the meeting. Judging from the looks from the others around her, she must have gasped. Some were looking in his direction trying to figure out what was wrong, but he could see Marshall behind her, looking directly at him. He, too, seemed taken aback.

The only thing to do now was to nod in the direction of the door and mouth, "I'll explain later." He could see she understood, but she made no attempt to respond. She simply looked away.

The first hour of the meeting passed without much attention being paid to it as Tandon's attention was drawn elsewhere. As the minutes passed, he grew increasingly disturbed. Every time he glanced in JulieAnn's direction, hoping to share a moment of eye contact, he received nothing. The looks he did receive were from Marshall, the man he had only met one time and who sat behind her glaring heatedly at him.

The chairman decided, after a time, to call for a, "twenty minute recess after which time we will begin to hear statements from both supporters and non-supporters alike." Out in the hall Tandon quickly found JulieAnn and headed toward her. When she saw him she stepped away from her group and met him. Tandon would have leaned in to kiss her but her demeanor warned against such an idea.

"What are you doing here?" she asked in a fierce whisper and rushed on. "I asked you if you wanted to come and you said no. Why are you here?

Why are you wearing that uniform? Why are you sitting with them?" She nearly spit the last out.

Tandon expected the surprise, actually he had expected a happier surprise, but this tension crackling from her was more than he had expected. "JulieAnn," he said and reached out to touch her, but she jerked away. He frowned, "I can explain."

"Okay. Explain," she demanded.

"I tried to call you. I wanted to tell you before you saw me here."

"You can tell me now," she said and crossed her arms defiantly.

Tandon was all nerves under her scrutinizing glare. "I had told you the truth. I wasn't planning on coming."

She raised her eyebrows at that.

"It's kind of a funny story." He tried to smile at that, but it felt flat, even to himself, and he could see it didn't do anything to reassure JulieAnn. "My old boss, Greg Zimmerman, came by my apartment. It seems he never filed my resignation. He thought I might really still want my job and wrote me a leave of absence instead."

JulieAnn's face softened at that. "He sounds like a nice boss. But did you explain that you really did mean to quit?"

"Yes, I did," he said. "Then he told me he needed me to testify."

She frowned, confused, "Why would he need you to do that?"

He knew how it would sound, but answered truthfully, "He didn't say." When he saw her mouth open and she turned her head away, he rushed to explain, "I think it has something to do with him. Maybe his job's on the line or something."

JulieAnn looked at him, an unreadable expression plaguing her features, then took a few steps away. After a moment she faced him and asked quietly, "I don't understand. I mean, I do understand that you'd want to help your boss," she put her fingers over her mouth for a moment then asked, "but how can you? I mean, I thought," she seemed at a loss for words. Tandon wished he could help her but wasn't exactly sure what she was asking. She stepped close to him then and touched his arm, smiling, "Tandon, you don't agree with them anymore. You said so yourself, remember? You're not on their side anymore. You're on ours. You'd be lying."

This time it was Tandon's turn to look shocked. "JulieAnn," he said, shaking his head, "I never said that."

She smiled consolingly," You probably just forgot, but..."

"No, JulieAnn, I know I never said that because it's not true." He saw a flicker of irritation flash across her face and added for confirmation, "I have always believed in this effort and always will." Suddenly JulieAnn looked lost, and Tandon could tell she was trying to remember.

"But you said you didn't see things the way you once had. Don't you remember? You used to believe in what they were doing to nationalize the river, but then you saw things differently. You changed your mind. That's why you quit."

Tandon was very uncomfortable now and ran

his hand through his hair. "JulieAnn, when I said I didn't see things the same anymore, I wasn't talking about the river. I didn't quit because of the river. I quit because of you."

JulieAnn's jaw dropped as despair spread across her face and Tandon explained quickly, "It's not your fault. I'm not blaming you. I'm saying it's because of you that things changed for me. I used to see my job in tunnel vision. It was all I focused on. You know all the things I've ruined because of it. But after seeing you last year," he flung his arm out, "when I went back to work, it was just…it was all different. Not the job or the Park Service, but me, I was different. I couldn't focus and I yelled at everyone. I was lost. But that's all changed now. I'm finally happy. You saved me."

They stood there, neither speaking, as JulieAnn conspicuously swiped at her cheeks and dabbed her eyes as she struggled for control of her emotions. Tandon wanted to take her in his arms but knew she wouldn't allow it, so they stood there silently until the call to return to the meeting was issued.

Automatically they turned to head in, then JulieAnn grabbed his arm, stopping him, "You can find your boss and tell him you changed your mind. We can follow through with the plans we already had. Nothing has to change."

Tandon could hear the desperation in her voice and thought he knew why. "JulieAnn, if you're still worried about your family, don't be. Remember, Jess came to me before he even knew I had quit. They wanted me to come back to you even though they thought I still worked for the Park."

"But they only did it for me. They only really came around when I told them why you quit."

"Well, we'll just have to explain it. Everything will be fine."

Greg found them then, "Tandon we have to go in now."

He nodded to Greg and he and JulieAnn walked slowly to the door. As they were about to part and go to their own seats, JulieAnn made one last plea, "Tandon, please, don't do it." Then, slowly, she turned and walked away.

* * *

JulieAnn tried valiantly to pay attention and take as many notes as possible. She had to keep telling herself to focus, she was here on business after all. Whenever she felt tears coming on she had to scold herself to regain her composure. And, for a while, that would work. Until a momentary lapse would draw her back into the pit of despair.

How could she have made such a mistake? Tandon was right, he had never actually said he'd changed his mind about the river. She had assumed that. Her eyes closed at the thought then flew open when she realized she had spread her misunderstanding around to her family, her friends, and oh, she sucked in her breath, Tandon's father. Her eyes darted to Tandon's, then away just as quickly when she saw him watching her. How was she ever going to explain this to Mr. Bowman? It would crush him, and worst of all, it would ruin their relationship.

Her heart breaking, JulieAnn tried desperately to focus as those in her group took their turns speaking on behalf of the landowners. This was their big moment and all she could do was hang on while her life spun out of control. Her mind and emotions seemed to be warring against one another. It doesn't matter, really, does it? Everyone likes him, and they'll be so pleased when they find out we're engaged, won't they? But that's only because they think differently of him now. Their minds would change back again if they knew. Maybe they won't have to know. But they will. Word will spread. So what! So what if he's still on the Park's side. It's our life anyway. Whose business is it anyway who I marry? It would strain my family. It would always be uncomfortable, and even confrontational, whenever we were together. And we'll need their support as Tandon's father would disown him again.

Her thoughts were torture. How could this be happening? It felt almost as if they were being forced apart by some evil plot. She felt near hysteria, a woman on the brink of losing everything. Every time she thought things were working out they weren't. It always ended badly. Why, she asked herself.

Suddenly a terrible thought pierced her and she gasped as her hand flew to her mouth. Was it true? Are we being forced apart? Are we not meant to be together? Then, just as suddenly, she had to stifle a giggle. How silly, she thought. She was just getting carried away. But the feeling persisted, growing stronger and stronger. A knot tightened in her stomach.

Then she heard it, Tandon's name spoken into a

speaker - his name and job title, and she froze. Somehow, instinctively, she knew, sensed, that what Tandon would say next would be the answer to her question. When, finally, the moment came, JulieAnn held her breath, her eyes fixated on the face of the only man she had ever loved, and she waited.

"Tandon Bowman," came the crisp tone, "do you, in your best estimation, agree that the land outlined in this bill does, indeed, qualify for inclusion into and deserves the protection of the National Park Service under the Department of the Interior?"

For a brief moment, when Tandon turned to look at her, JulieAnn felt a glimmer of hope. She had asked him, before taking her seat, not to go through with it. Maybe he would change his mind, even now, at the last minute. But then her vision cleared and she saw the sorrow, the apology, in his eyes before he turned away and spoke into the microphone, "I agree."

* * *

"JulieAnn," she felt a touch on her arm, "it's time to go."

"Oh," she breathed, dazed. She looked down into her lap where her reporting tools lay and bent to pick up her bag to put them away. Unzipping it, she was drawn to the large envelope, and slowly removed it. It's true, she thought, we aren't meant to be. And at that moment it all made sense.

Wearily, she stood, following the crowd out the door. She walked on, unaware of where she was going, until Tandon's voice stopped her. She looked up at him and saw the hope, the apology - saw the words he spoke, but she couldn't hear them from the pounding in her ears. She simply and silently handed him the envelope, then turned and walked to the bus as tears washed, unchecked, down her cheeks.

EPILOGUE

There was always something special about watching the sunset, Tandon thought, as he leaned against the chimney overlooking the hills and mountains. It created a sense of peace, a quietness that his soul longed for, and offered a rare moment of reflection - of closure. Tonight though, Tandon sensed it even more. Perhaps it was due to the soft glow of pinks and purples spread across the sky. His mother had always told him it meant the next day would be beautiful... a special gift from God. And he had always believed her. He still did.

The light was fading and Tandon leaned away from the chimney to remove his wallet from his pocket. He opened it, as he had for years, but more so lately, to pull out the well-worn photo within. It was a large photo and he had folded it so many times that there were faded creases throughout it, but it didn't bother him. To him it was as clear as the day it was taken. He could still feel the cool breeze from the waterfall behind them, the breathless kiss that followed, and he remembered the love, the fulfillment, he felt at that moment.

He turned it over then to read what was left of the note, though unnecessarily as it was engraved, long ago, upon his heart.

For the only man I have ever loved...a memento.
Let's always love like this.
Forever,
JulieAnn

With great care, Tandon refolded it, putting it back into his wallet for safe keeping. Since the day JulieAnn had given him the envelope he had never let the picture out of his sight.

The sun was passing below the horizon, and with the light that remained he rose, with some consideration for his weary body, and found his bedding. As darkness settled in, the stars grew in number as Tandon lay on his back, watching them flicker, too many to count. He recalled hearing recently that though we could see the stars with the naked eye, many were so far away that it would take more than a lifetime to ever reach them. The thought made him pause then, as it did now, to think how much was really out there, and how small we really are. Yet, despite that, we are not insignificant. A lump of emotion tightened in his chest, and hot tears slid back across his temples. It was hard for him to swallow that knowing the only significant thing he had ever done was to use his influence. It had been his only way of apologizing.

As predicted would happen, Congress did

establish the Buffalo National River on March 1, 1972. Immediately, in the days that followed, Tandon called Greg and fairly demanded that his father and JulieAnn's grandparents be given the Life Estate plan, and he kept on Greg until the day they were approved. Still, it had brought him no consolation. Nothing had. He had spent the rest of his career with the Park Service moving around every two years, unwilling to stay in one place any longer than that. He was never willing, or able, to be in a serious relationship and so never married, nor had children of his own. He always wondered, though, about JulieAnn, whether she married and had her own family, but he never tried to find out. It would have hurt too much to know. He hoped, with all of his heart, though, that she was happy. He couldn't have stood it if she weren't. He never contacted his father either. He knew his father would call him a coward, and he was probably right. In the end he knew the best thing was to move on. They would forget about him soon enough and go on with their lives as usual. He thought he would too, and yet, here he was, needing some kind of closure.

Tandon turned his head to the side and saw the shadow of his mother's daffodils near him. It was funny, he thought, that for some people, like his mother, life could be so rewarding. Then, for others, it was such a struggle. He wondered what put a person in a certain category. Was it their upbringing? Their faith? Maybe they were just born able to tough it out. He remembered the peace on her face in those last days that he saw her. And though she was dying, she had more strength than either he or his father ever had. He wondered what her secret was.

He remembered her words to him then, "Forget what he is and love him for who he is." Was that what she did? Not caring so much about what someone did but simply who he was. Was her husband just that, her husband and he, her son? Was it as simple as that?

Tandon looked up into the sky then as tears began to fall. Maybe, all of these years, when he'd been weighed down by the things he had done, he should have been more concerned about who he was. He was a man like any other, with passions and dreams and needs like all others. And he was someone who made mistakes like everyone else. Now, perhaps, it was time to let go of the past - the guilt. Time to stop dwelling on what he could have been, or done, and just be himself.

He had only one regret that wouldn't be let go that easily. And that was JulieAnn. He had loved her with a passion he had never known before or since. And if he'd had a choice for something to have worked out, it would have been to have had a life with her. He would have given her the moon if he could have. But it wasn't meant to be. He would always love her though, like no other.

Tandon took the picture back out of his wallet, preparing to let it go. Their love was real once, but it was time to move on. Without warning, he felt a crushing pressure in his chest and clutched himself, falling to his side. Another came then, and he gritted his teeth in pain. He lay back, unable to focus on anything but the knowledge that he must be having a heart attack, when it began to subside.

For a moment he panicked knowing he couldn't call for help and knowing that no one knew where he was. Then, recalling his new outlook, a welcoming peace settled over him, and he smiled. If this was where he was meant to die, then this is where he would die. Here at home, in his old room, smelling the sweet smell of his mother's flowers, and with the heavenly view above.

Tandon's smile remained with him for a time, until the next pain took it, the picture still clenched tightly in his hand.

* * *

JulieAnn woke with a start. Unsure whether it was a sound she had heard, she lay still, listening. She heard nothing. Rolling over to her side, she looked out the window. It was a cool night, but the crickets and frogs were out in full force. Probably, she thought, what woke her up. They could get so noisy at times, she grinned.

She pushed the sheet back, being careful not to move too much, and got up to close the window, but when she reached it something stopped her. She looked out into the pitch black night. She didn't think anything or anyone was there, though. It was more a feeling she got within her, a sense that something wasn't right.

She looked up to the sky, alight with twinkling stars. A shiver ran through her then, and she hugged her arms about her. At that moment a face she hadn't seen in a long time came to her. She could see Tandon just as clearly as if he stood in front of her.

A warmth enveloped her then, and she closed her eyes. She felt a deep sadness overwhelm her, and when she finally opened them unshed tears spilled down her cheeks. She began to sob then, quietly, so as not to wake Marshall. She had thought about Tandon throughout the years, not constantly, but every now and again when something would bring him to mind. Tonight, out of the blue like this, she knew something had happened.

Though their lives had taken different paths, she had always loved Tandon, always felt a special connection to him that, sadly, she could never share with her husband, though she loved him with all her heart. And tonight, she knew instinctively, that her love was gone. Quietly, she said a prayer to God, hoping that he had found happiness - that his life had had purpose, and she thanked Tandon for what he had done for her grandparents. She knew, without a doubt, that it was because of him that her beloved grandparents were able to die in their home. She knew, too, that he had done the same for his father. Despite the hurt his father had felt, Isaac Bowman had died, grateful, to his only son. The son he still loved and missed.

Finally, when there were no tears left, she looked out of the window into the clear, black, starry night, and said goodbye one last time.

Tammy Snyder lives in the Ozark Mountains of Arkansas with her husband and children.
If you enjoyed her story, please leave a review or email her at:
tamssnyder@yahoo.com

Made in the USA
Columbia, SC
04 July 2024